Born To Be Hurt

The rose symbolizes love, depair and the need for forgiveness. It was apparantly Gary's sole means of communication.

All characters appearing in the novel are fictitious. Any resemblance to real persons, living or dead, is purely coincidental.

To order additional copies, please contact us.
BookSurge, LLC
www.booksurge.com
1-866-308-6235
orders@booksurge.com

MARIELLE O'CONNOR MOSLEY

BORN TO BE HURT

2006

Born To Be Hurt

To Joe & Margaret
My Prayers are with
you Praying for quick
recovery and good health
for many years to come.
Enjoy!
Marielle Mosley

ACKNOWLEDGEMENT

I would like to thank my son Michael O'Connor who throughout the years urged me to do something with my book. This encouraged me to keep it uppermost in my mind. I had to have <u>Born To Be Hurt</u> published 'some time' in the future.

My sister Dolores Guerrier who is responsible for editing and getting my novel published.

I wish to dedicate this book to my beloved deceased husband John O'Connor Sr. He encouraged and provided me the time and opportunity to pursue my desire to write.

I also want to dedicate this book to all of my children who are my pride and joy. I especially want to remember my deceased son John Jr. His untimely death gave me insight into the depth and sorrow of a grieving mother. This experience helped me to understand pain and suffering and gave me the ability to empathize with people.

PROLOGUE

This is the story of Melanie Daniels. She told me the tragic details of her life. She was humiliated, beaten, tortured and finally suffered a tragic ending.

Human nature is so complex. The fine line between sanity and insanity cannot always be distinguished. Many people endure insufferable pain with no thought of retaliation. Do certain souls have to compensate for the gift of sensitivity by having to endure the most tragic hurts? Must an individual who experiences the whole gamut of human emotions soar to the top of the mountain of exhilarating moments only to be plummeted to the valley of despair and humiliation.

This book is not an analysis of Melanie's life. It is based on the tragic life of my friend. She was a fine, sensitive and compassionate person, loved by everyone. She was too naïve. Melanie was a fun loving person who enjoyed life and who suffered the worst kinds of tragedies. She was *BORN TO BE HURT.*

Laurie Casey

-1-

MELANIE SPEAKS
(AS TOLD TO LAURIE CASEY)

I took it upon myself to go and have a talk with Gary's mother, Irene Daniels, my mother-in-law. I didn't know how to approach her, so I made small talk and nonchalantly questioned her about Gary's childhood. She was a little uneasy, but it was evident that she loved him. She told me,

"I was worried when I carried Gary because I was so old. I was afraid he wouldn't be normal. The doctors assured me that Gary was fine. He was amazed with his progress. Gary was advanced physically and intellectually, however, he was a loner. He had no friends and he seemed to want it just that way."

"Did he ever have severe headaches? Did he go into rages and have temper tantrums?" I asked

"Well, I never!" She replied. "What are you insinuating? Do you think that I raised a monster? If you're having problems with him or if he's having headaches and going into rages, most likely you're to blame. What nerve!"

She was hysterical. I couldn't believe what she was saying. It was too much for me to bear. I started to cry and ran out of the house. I was extremely upset. I went home and started to think about all of the tragedies in my life. I had to talk to someone. I decided to confide in Laurie.

We were brought up in a small town in Camden, Maine. I was the youngest of four children. We lived in a poor section of town. Our house was very tiny and cluttered. The outside needed paint. There was no grass and the yard was filled with useless junk that my brothers and father had collected.

Dad was a dreamer who had no other ambition in life than to drink most of the time. He couldn't hold a job.

I was petrified of my father, especially when he came home drunk at night. I was afraid that he would come into my room smelling of booze and try to fondle me. I felt sick to my stomach when my mother left him as the baby-sitter. He got pleasure out of making me cry by making fun of me or by hitting me. I think he was taking out his frustrations on me.

My mother was so busy trying to make ends meet she had no time for us. She was the sole provider. She couldn't count on my father. I can still see her tired and unhappy face. I can't recall ever seeing any display of affection between my parents. I felt sorry for myself. I was alone and unloved.

I was a very petite blond haired child. People say that I was pretty, but that I had big poignant brown eyes. They looked like the eyes of a doe beautiful but sad.

As the years passed, we were busy with our chores that included house, yard, and schoolwork. Mother never said anything. She just shouted out orders. If we hesitated she made us move. She would use the strap on us, whenever she thought it was necessary which was often. My mother was a good person but she did not have the ability to communicate with us. I could not approach her with my problems or questions. She had a 'don't bother me' attitude. So I never 'bothered' her.

I loved to sneak down by the old water works and just daydream. This was my favorite pastime. My dream was always the same one: 'I was loved by a tall, dark and handsome man.' I imagined myself being in a grandiose home with four children to love. 'Love them,' I would. I knew I would shower them with affection and understanding, something I had never had. The promise that I made to myself gave me the courage to continue to do my best.

I didn't have any friends and that bothered me. I had no time to cultivate friendships. I couldn't have brought anyone to my house anyhow. I was too busy, had too many chores and school work to do. I was easily taken advantage of and I was an easy target for ridicule. I was extremely sensitive and cried at the drop of a hat.

I was alone most of the time. I felt so depressed. How I longed to have someone with whom I could share my secrets. I never had a close friend so I created an imaginary one. I would talk to her and tell her my problems. This helped me to cope with my everyday stress.

I remember when I started menstruating. I had no idea what was happening to me. I had never heard anything about this subject. I was so frightened that I waited one whole day before I approached my mother. I thought something horrible was happening to me. I was not quite sure what it was. My mother just handed me a box of sanitary napkins and taught me how to put them on. She was indifferent as she said that I now was a 'big girl' and therefore, I would have to stay away from boys because I could get pregnant. She never told me how I could get pregnant. She just warned me not to. As I was leaving the room, she told me to expect this to happen every month. She added that it was a curse women had to learn to accept.

I had so much to learn about life and the 'facts' of life. I decided to start hanging around the gangs at school. I made sure that I took everything in. I didn't understand most of the jokes at first, but I laughed anyway. I slowly became a little more street smart. I started to read *True Romances*. I would get pretty excited and aroused at some of the things I read. I felt pretty hip and thought that I knew everything.

Over the years, I stayed in my own little world. I was the only child left at home but I was forced to leave school and go earn my room and board, as my siblings had done. My sister was unhappily married. My oldest brother was married and lived away from home. My other two brothers had moved away as soon as they had to quit school to go to work.

We were never close. We lived in the same house but shared nothing. Once my brothers moved out I hardly ever saw them again. Once in a while, my sister visited my parents.

I was pretty proud of myself. At the age of sixteen, I had a good paying job in one of the better mills in town. I was a good worker. I liked my job. I even made many friends. We never went out together, but we shared our lunches and coffee breaks. I thought that was grand. For the first time in my life I was happy. No one could take this away from me.

I will never forget one particular occasion. Three months after I had been working, they hired a new boy. I distinctly remember the first time I saw him. My heart jumped. I was glad he hadn't seen me because my face must have been beet red. I was a little surprised that I was losing it over one boy after one look. He was so handsome...tall dark...and he had the biggest blue eyes. He was my dream man! I got all of this knowledge from one glance. I made my way to my workbench and got busy. I was so nervous I couldn't work properly. I told myself to stop it. I didn't have a chance. I could hear all the girls cooing over him. They had an advantage over me. They were not shy. Jeanne, a cute little redhead was already introducing herself to him. I knew that I could never bring myself to do that.

As I busied myself with my work, I raised my eyes and caught him starring at me. He smiled and I dropped my tools on the floor. I was so embarrassed. I didn't know what to do. He came over to me and introduced himself. His name was Gary Daniels. He told me that he thought I was beautiful.

"Thank you, I'm Melanie Webster."

That's all we said to each other. The next day, I caught him starring at me. This time I handled the situation a little bit more maturely. He had such an effect on me and I loved every minute of it. I was still getting shivers just from the sight of him. Was this normal? I didn't dare ask anyone for fear that it wasn't. I was so proud! He had chosen me.

At lunchtime, Gary sat with me. It was a sight that raised more than one eyebrow. I told myself:

"Slow down Melanie, he's only having lunch with you."

He asked if he could drive me home. I refused. I was too worried about what my mother would say. So I told Gary the truth. He said:

"What if I drop you off at the corner of your street?"

I should have refused. I had never disobeyed my parents before. I couldn't explain the feelings that this guy brought out in me. I wondered if he could detect them. I didn't care. I felt so carefree and giddy. He was paying attention to ME. I accepted the ride. He once again told me I was the prettiest girl he had ever seen. He didn't try to kiss me. He asked me if he could take me out on a date. I told him that I would have to check with my parents. As much as I wanted to go out with Gary I couldn't muster up enough courage to ask my mother.

I went to bed early that night in anticipation of the following day. It finally came and I made it to work. My heart was racing. There he was, waiting for me with a great big smile. I was the happiest girl in the world.

At lunchtime, he asked me to go out with him. I was so nervous I didn't know what to say. I could probably meet him at Kippy's, a dance hall, where I was allowed to go on Friday nights. When I suggested this to him, his face stiffened. He said he didn't like dancing. I didn't know what to say. There was silence for a moment but he said he'd meet me at the dance hall.

I was so nervous all week. I actually made myself physically sick. This was my very first date. Finally the big night came. I was one of the first ones to arrive at Kippy's. I kept looking for Gary. He wasn't there so I panicked. I was sure he had changed his mind. It was nine o'clock and he still hadn't arrived. I felt like crying. I hadn't told anyone about Gary. No one knew I had been stood up. I waited until ten fifteen and decided to leave. I had never felt so hurt and humiliated in my life. I was glad no one talked to me because I would have burst into tears.

As I was walking home, tears were rolling down my face. I didn't care. I was so super sensitive. I wanted to kick myself for crying but I couldn't help it. All of a sudden a car pulled alongside of me, it was Gary.

"I'm sorry Mel, I told you I hate dance halls."

""What a weird statement!" I thought.

"That doesn't give you the right to stand me up."

"I said I was sorry." He angrily replied. "Please, get in the car and we'll talk."

I continued walking. He stopped the car, jumped out and stood in front of me. He put his hands on my shoulders and looked into my eyes with his big blue eyes. That was it! Our lips met in the most tender, most intimate way. It still thrills me as I tell you about it.

I was probably wrong, but at that moment I knew I was in love with a man I knew nothing about. I could not tear myself away from him. I remember thinking it was a good thing we were not in the car. Anything could have happened. Finally, I came to my senses and pushed him away. Good god! We were on the sidewalk. I'd really have something to worry about if someone had seen us and reported it to my mother. Luckily no one was there. I had a need to invent things to worry about.

A few days passed and I was convinced that nobody had seen us. I was safe. Things were seemingly quiet around the house. My father had been diagnosed with cancer of the liver and he didn't have much longer to live. I felt sorry for him. I neither loved nor hated him. I probably was like him. I was an easy pushover. He never had the courage to stand up to my mother. He chose to drink and take out his frustration on me because I was so little and afraid of him. He didn't dare pick on anyone else because they would retaliate and he knew it. When he was drunk he abused me. He was a coward, a man who lived a wasted life.

Monday finally arrived. I couldn't wait to see Gary. I had relived the 'kiss' all weekend. There he was waiting for me. He put his arms around me. I couldn't help feeling a little pride as everyone stared at us. I could almost hear the girls whispering:

"Boy, is she lucky."

Was I? I sure felt like it. Gary asked me if I would see him that night. I didn't know how I could manage it because it was a Monday night and the stores were closed. I couldn't tell my mother that I was going to the store. I told him I'd talk to my mother and see him the following night.

I got up enough nerve to approach my mother. It wasn't too bad. In fact she didn't show any emotion at all. She didn't even question me about Gary. I wouldn't have known what to tell her since I didn't know much about him except that he was handsome. She told me I could see him once during the week and twice on weekends. I couldn't believe it! My mother had mellowed.

Our dating officially started. On our first date we just rode around, stopped for milkshakes and talked. I was relieved when he didn't try to kiss me. We talked about each other and I discovered that Gary was more of a loner than I was. As I listened to him talk and observed him, I noticed that he occasionally stared into space. That frightened me. Then he would say something romantic and I'd forget about the staring incident. He was careful not to move too quickly in the relationship. He kissed me goodnight but with restraint. I was relieved because I just wanted him to hold me in his arms.

Gary was extremely possessive and moody. For no apparent reason he would go into a depression and get the same blank stare that had previously frightened me. This didn't happened too often, so I just shrugged it off.

He wanted to have more than a platonic relationship. I had a hard time holding him back. Let's face it I didn't really want to hold back. It was so hard to resist him but I definitely didn't want to get pregnant. I just knew I wanted to stay in his arms forever. Gary knew this and he had such a way about him that he won me over. I don't know where he had learned to make love, but to me it was magical. I didn't feel any guilt or shame. Finally I was loved and I belonged to someone who cared. I was someone who mattered. Reality set in and I was afraid of getting pregnant.

I was afraid of my mother, but Gary told me I was his forever. He wanted to marry me. He said,

"I want to marry you. I know it's too soon but I don't care. I know you feel the same way about me. What we share together is something very rare. The way you respond to me proves that you feel the same way."

I said,

"Stop it! You're embarrassing me."

"Mel, I'm only trying to tell you that what we shared is unique. Our love is a rare gift coming from the depths of our being. We are meant to be together forever. We have to get married."

He was so convincing; however, I knew my mother would never agree.

"Gary, I'm only sixteen."

"So what! I'm twenty-one and you're mature for your age. We'll elope. Please Mel, tell me you'll marry me. We'll elope. I've got to be with you forever. I'm so alone. Life without you is not worth living."

I couldn't believe my ears. This gorgeous man was crying and pleading with ME. I agreed to marry him and to elope. After my decision, I was more relaxed.

We continued to date and make love. The nights that we didn't spend together were miserable and lonely. He had completely captured my heart, mind, and soul. As the time for our elopement approached, I started having doubts. My feelings for him wavered between extreme blind love and fear.

He would go into rages for no reason. A couple of times he slapped me across the face. He then cried like a baby and begged me to forgive him. He couldn't explain his actions. He said he was so afraid I would not marry him that it made him extremely nervous and irrational. He was afraid of losing me. He was sure he would have no reason to feel so insecure and uptight after we were married. I believed him. A few days after this episode we went for blood tests.

On the day that we were to elope, Gary came to tell me that I would have to stay an hour longer. I worked the extra hour, but Gary had to stay longer. I decided to go home and he could come to get me later. I kissed him and told him that I would see him in the evening. It was raining when I left. A coworker offered to give me a ride home. I had known Bob for many years and he was a nice person. Gary watched us leave. He followed us, pushed me out of the way and punched Bob. Bob defended himself and pinned Gary to the ground. He was about to beat Gary to a pulp, but for my sake he restrained himself. Bob looked at me and said:

"Something is terribly wrong with your friend. He should see a doctor and have his head examined."

Then he got up and left abruptly. I cried and shouted,

"I never want to see you again. Get out of my life and stay out."

I didn't sleep that night. I felt so lonely and betrayed. I felt that there was no reason to go on living. I knew I couldn't live with Gary, but I also knew I couldn't go on without him. What was I going to do? I didn't want to go to work, but on the other hand I did not want to stay home with my father. I no longer feared him but I still felt uneasy in his presence. Finally, I decided to go to work. I would just ignore Gary.

I rounded the corner to the work place, and I saw Gary. He looked as though he had not slept at all. We just stared at each other. He cried,

"Oh! Melanie, I'm so sorry, I love you so much. Please, forgive me."

He embraced me. I was lost in his arms. The loneliness, the pain and the humiliation of the previous day no longer existed. I was not rational. I was hopelessly in love. I was going to marry Gary and live with him for the rest of my life.

We got into his car and made our way to the bank where he withdrew some money. We called in sick and made our way to city hall in the next town. We were married and then went to tell my parents about the 'good' news. My mother screamed and yelled that I was a most ungrateful child. She told me I was no better than the rest of the family members who were utterly selfish and self-centered.

"The minute you start to earn money, you decide to leave your father and me with all the chores and the bills. Let me tell you, young lady, if you leave now, I never want to see you again."

Married life agreed with me. Gary adored me and treated me like a queen. He smothered me with affection, attention and passion. Sometimes, however, I felt as though I was his possession and I feared his possessiveness. A few times during the middle of the night I would catch him just sitting there staring at me. When I questioned him, he didn't recall any of this but he did remember that he had had a nightmare and a terrible headache.

Our apartment was special because Gary and I had spent a great deal of time fixing it to our liking. Gary was very talented. He excelled in everything he attempted to do. He certainly was not lazy. I just loved to watch him work or just fix things around the house. We were happy. I was so proud of our little apartment. I wanted to invite my friends from work, share my happiness, and have them spend an evening with us.

When I suggested this to Gary, he turned ashen white. He put his arms around me and said,

"Not yet, Mel, after all we're still newlyweds."

He started kissing me in the neck. He continued to caress, fondle and arouse me. We stood naked in the middle of the kitchen. He laughed and said,

"See honey, we don't have time for friends. We have each other."

I agreed. I was so crazy about him. I would have done anything to please him.

"You are so wonderful in bed, Mel. The thought of you ever bringing this much joy to any other man, makes me want to kill you."

I was a little stunned by his remark but I took it in stride. I accepted it as a compliment. I did say to him,

"Is that what my lovemaking does to you? I must be doing something wrong for you to be thinking such dark thoughts."

"No, please, forget what I said. I couldn't bear to see you change anything. Sometimes I say crazy things without even thinking. It has nothing to do with you. I have always been that way."

He took me in his arms and we made love again. We fell asleep.

After a few months, I wondered why I wasn't pregnant. I secretly wished that I were but I didn't want to mention it to Gary. I knew he didn't like to talk about the possibility of a child. He said I was the only baby he ever wanted.

Life went on as usual. Gary and I worked and enjoyed the togetherness. We left for work together in the morning; shared our lunch and coffee breaks; and came home for dinner. I loved preparing his meal, as he read the newspaper.

Gary was an industrious and talented worker. He was promoted to assistant plant manager. I was so proud of him that I wanted to celebrate. I prepared a surprise party for him at our apartment. I thought to myself,

"He won't mind. We are no longer newlyweds."

I had so much fun planning and organizing the party. It was my first party and I wanted it to be perfect for Gary. I tried to hide all the evidence so that he wouldn't get suspicious. I succeeded.

That night the guests had arrived before Gary came home. As he came into the apartment they all shouted,

"Surprise, surprise!"

Much to my dismay, I saw that Gary's face was distorted. His eyes were wide and blank. I had seen this expression before. No one seemed to notice it. They were having such a good time, mingling, eating, and drinking. The food and the decorations were beautiful and the guests complimented me. Gary was downright rude. He stayed in the corner of the room sulking. Finally, he got up from his chair and yelled,

"I want everyone to leave now. It's past my bedtime."

He left the room abruptly and went into his bedroom. I was shocked and I apologized as best as I could. My guests were civil and tried to make light of the situation. I thanked them as they all left. I was so ashamed, hurt, and embarrassed. I sat in the kitchen and just cried. Tears of shame turned into tears of rage. I marched into the bedroom and screamed,

"How dare you embarrass me in front of the only friends I have ever had. Who the hell do you think you are? Where do you come off being rude to those nice people, you bastard? I have had it with you."

I couldn't believe I had said this. I was afraid as I saw that gazed look on my husband's face. I started to back away as he came toward me. I didn't recognize him He was unlike the man I had married. He smashed me across the mouth and I fell to the floor. He started ripping my clothes off until I was nude. His face was filled with irrational, uncontrollable passion. I am ashamed to admit this but he aroused me and soon my passion equaled his. Just as I was ready to climax, he stood over me, masturbated, laughed, and left the room. What a sick, pathetic scene.

The following day, I was afraid to talk about the events of the previous night with Gary. I relegated it to the back of my mind as I had with the rest of our unresolved problems. Gary never mentioned it either. I was too timid to say anything, but I knew something was terribly wrong with Gary and our relationship. He acted as though nothing had ever happened and so I forgot about it.

Nothing changed. I decided I would forgo any attempt to have friends. It was easier to give in to Gary's whims and avoid his rages and beatings. I loved and feared him at the same time. I could not bear the thought of having to live without him so I did nothing about his moods and I stayed and endured them. We continued to live the charade of a 'normal' life.

We had been married three years, and had no children. At first we made sure we didn't make love without protection. After three years, Gary took it for granted that I couldn't have children, so he was careless; however, I had not given up on the idea of becoming a mother. I thought that having a child would make my life more meaningful and it would help me be less miserable. I didn't dare mention this to Gary. I remembered my dream as a child and I knew I wanted to become a mother and someday my wish would become a reality.

A few months went by and I still was not pregnant. I decided to make an appointment with a doctor for a consultation. I had to lie to Gary, so I told him that I was not feeling well and I needed to see a doctor. He was not too pleased with the idea. The thought that someone else would touch me infuriated him. We had a terrible argument. Finally I told him I might be suffering from something very serious, but to satisfy him I wouldn't go to the doctor. I told him my condition could worsen but then he would be well rid of me. I added,

"Don't give me this business about loving me and not being able to live without me. If you loved me, you would want me to take care of myself."

He yelled,

"Shut up you spoiled brat. Go to your fancy doctor and let him fondle you. You are nothing but an oversexed maniac."

"You're sick Gary. I will choose an old doctor. I know an old and ugly one."

I ruffled his hair and made a joke about his reaction. I knew he was serious. He was extremely jealous and on the verge of tears.

The doctor who was 'young and handsome' put me through a battery of tests and assured me I was in excellent condition and should be able to bear as many children as I wanted. He then told me I should have my husband checked. I gasped and told him that was not possible. I told him my husband didn't want any children and if he knew why I had really come to see him he would kill me. I told him I had to lie to my husband and added that I had described the doctor as 'old and decrepit. The doctor quickly said:

"My! My! Young lady you have a very serious problem. I wouldn't advise you to bring a child into this world with the kind of situation you have at home. A child should be wanted by both parents."

There was no way I would consider his advice. I desperately wanted a baby and I really thought a child would make a difference and improve our relationship.

I was so obsessed with this matter that I decided to go see a psychologist. I proceeded to tell him about my dilemma and he said to me:

"It is hard for me to advise you. From what you have told me, I think that your husband would benefit from some professional help. Deep down your husband knows he has a problem. It might be something that can be simply remedied with medication. For some unknown reason, he is terrified. I think it is very important that you convince him to come to see me."

I knew the doctor was right, but Gary didn't even know I had gone to see a psychologist. How could I mention it without sending him into a blind rage? I just had to forget about my hopes and continue life as usual.

We were heading home from work one night, and Gary was acting strangely. He was fidgety and nervous. I could tell he wanted to tell me something. I couldn't figure out what it was but I knew I couldn't ask him. I would have to wait for him to tell me when he was ready.

After dinner he helped me with the dishes. He rarely did this, so I was convinced that what he had to tell me was very important. He didn't appear to be angry. I knew it wasn't bad news. After we had finished in the kitchen, Gary took my hand and led me to the couch. He then told me he had wonderful news.

"Mel, I got a huge promotion today. I am going to be the manager."

"That's wonderful news," I replied. "Why did you wait so long to tell me? I'd think that you'd be so proud and happy that you couldn't keep it to yourself.

"I am, but I'll no longer be in our department."

"So?" I replied

He yelled,

"I knew you'd take that attitude. Glad to be rid of me. Now I won't be able to keep an eye on you all day long. I have news for you, young lady. I will be earning a substantial amount of money so there won't be any need for you to work anymore. You will give your two-week notice as of Monday morning – and that's final! There's plenty of work for you to do around here."

I fooled him. I agreed with him. Little did he know that I wanted to get pregnant. I would eventually have to quit my job. I let him think he was the strong and wise man of the house and replied,

"Yes, dear if that's what you want. I'll give my notice Monday."

He looked puzzled and perhaps suspicious so I decided to change the subject.

uh

It was difficult to try to get pregnant without raising Gary's suspicion. I followed the doctor's advice and took my temperature every morning. When it was elevated, I seduced him and that wasn't too difficult. He wondered about the transformation because he was usually the one who initiated intimacy. He didn't complain he just profited of these occasions and said it made him feel important and powerful.

I was delighted when I discovered I was pregnant. I had to break the news to Gary. I was extremely nervous after I got the confirmation from the doctor that I was two months pregnant. I decided to prepare his favorite dinner. We would dine in the romantic setting of candlelight and soft music.

Gary came home from work and was passionately excited when he saw the dinner, the candlelight, and the music. He mistook my intentions, swept me up and brought me into the bedroom. We were lost in our lovemaking and forgot about dinner. As we lay there content and seemingly oblivious to any outside problems, I whispered to him:

"We're going to have a baby Out of our great love for each other we created a baby. Isn't this great?"

His body jerked and he jumped out of bed.

"Love, shit! You mean lust for your boyfriend."

"Gary, I'm not going to argue with you. You know this baby is yours. You're not man enough to accept responsibility. You can only insult and hurt me. You are nothing but a mean and selfish individual." I replied.

"You think your pregnancy makes you powerful and important? If you want me to support you and that kid of yours you will have to abide by my rules or I'll throw you both out." He screamed

I didn't say another word as I went to clean out the dining room which was supposed to have been a romantic getaway.

"What a sick psychotic man. "I thought.

I was foolish and naïve enough to believe that a child would make him more sympathetic and human. My pregnancy did manage to change a few things around the house. Gary no longer beat me or throw tantrums. He became silent and sullen and didn't help with any of the chores around the house. I didn't care because the knowledge of my baby growing inside of me filled me with peace and contentment. As far as I was concerned, I had it all.

One Saturday afternoon, Gary very nicely said to me:

"Put your sweater on honey. We are going for a ride. I've got something to show you."

"Where are you taking me?" I replied.

"You'll see." He said, as he drove up the driveway of a huge older house.

"Who lives here?" I asked.

"We will, very soon."

I didn't know how to react. On the one hand I was hurt because he hadn't consulted me and on the other hand I was delighted at the prospect of having a house to call our own.

"It's so big and the land is so rocky. There's no grass and there are no flowers."

"Don't you have any imagination, Mel? Can't you picture what it will look like after we have decorated and fixed it up? Look down the road, at the ocean. There's a private beach. What more could we want? All this will be our very own."

Gary had said 'our' very own. I was so thrilled. He had included me and maybe the baby, but I didn't want to mention it and break the spell. I didn't want him to know how I felt about his rejection of the baby so I said nothing. I just wanted to savor the moment for God knows when it would happen again. I just told him this was a very good move. I was happy and bitter at the same time. I was beginning to see and accept my husband as he really was.

Our house was a huge nine-room house built on several acres. I couldn't imagine why Gary wanted such a big house as he had repeatedly told me he didn't want any children. He didn't want any brats destroying his house. I was *all* that he wanted. Was he in for a surprise!

My pregnancy was uneventful. We were so busy remodeling and moving I was unable to share the joys of pending motherhood with Gary. Every time I mentioned anything pertaining to the baby, he totally ignored me. When I asked him to help me choose a name he said disdainfully:

"It's your baby, you pick out your own name."

Strangely enough, he never complained when I bought things for the baby. I never knew what his reactions would be. He surely was an enigma. I learned to accept him and therefore avoid many arguments.

I liked our new town. Everyone was so friendly. I met the girl who became my best friend at the supermarket. We were walking in the aisle and bumped into each other. We were both very pregnant. We looked at each other and started laughing. We introduced ourselves. Her name was Laurie and she was expecting her child one month after my child was due. She was a pretty blond girl who seemed to like me. We met a few times after that and I knew we would become good friends. She invited me to her home to have coffee. I accepted and spent a great afternoon with Laurie. I made sure I got home on time to get dinner ready for Gary. I didn't even tell him about my new friend.

One morning, as Gary was getting ready for work, I asked him to stay with me. I told him I had had a terrible night and I thought the baby would be born that day. I was three weeks overdue and I didn't feel well.

"What! Miss work so that I can hold your hand? You've had those pains before and it didn't mean anything. You'll be fine!"

He kissed me on the forehead and left. I had a horrible day. I had labor pains on and off all day, but not regularly. I didn't call the doctor. In the evening the pains came more frequently so I called the doctor. He told me to wait until the pains were closer and then get to the hospital and he would meet me there. It was six o'clock and Gary was not home yet.

I began to panic. I knew I had to get to the hospital and I couldn't drive myself, the pains were too strong. I was afraid of waiting any longer so I put my coat on and drove to my girlfriend's house. I rang the doorbell and a friendly gentleman answered. He was a mild mannered good-looking man. He was so different from my husband. Jack, Laurie's husband, and Laurie were so nice to me that I almost forgot the urgency of my visit. Laurie put on her coat and said to me:

"Come on Melanie we'll both take you to the hospital."

On our way to the hospital, Jack asked me if my husband was due home in the evening. I told him he had been delayed on the job and that he would be home later.

"Well that's good. Give me your telephone number and I'll call him to let him know where you are."

I panicked. I couldn't give him Gary's number. I couldn't take a chance. Gary might accuse him of being the father. I lied and told Jack I had left a message at his office letting him know where I was and to tell him to meet me at the hospital.

They stayed with me until I was settled in. Laurie hugged me and wished me good luck. She gave me her telephone number and told me to call her if I needed anything. I wondered if she suspected anything. Maybe she had heard talk around town about Gary and me. That couldn't be. Nobody in town even knew us. After I filled out all of the forms they wheeled me into the delivery room.

During the evening, I delivered a beautiful seven pound five ounce baby boy. I couldn't wait for Gary to come in. I was still the ultimate optimist. The doctor told me that he was going to call Gary. He never came. I was disillusioned, hurt and tired.

"Maybe he'll come tomorrow." I thought.

He never came. I didn't know what to do. I had to get all of the personal items from the hospital because nobody had brought any for me. I talked to Laurie on the telephone and pretended that everything was fine. I notified my family and they couldn't come. I also called Gary's parents and they came to see me one afternoon. We didn't have much to say to each other; however, Gary's mother did say that the baby resembled Gary. How I wished Gary could have heard her say this. My stay in the hospital was a painful, lonesome and sad time for me. There was one glimmer of light when I received a long stemmed rose from Gary, I presumed. It was an experience that I would never forget.

It was time for me to go home and I had no idea how I was going to get there. I had no choice but to call Gary. I didn't have any clothes. My heart was pounding as I called him. He answered the phone very brusquely.

"Hello!" I said. "Thank you for the rose. Would you come to get us tomorrow? Don't forget my suitcase. It's in the closet. It contains the baby's things and my clothes. Thank you."

"What time?" He replied.

"Eleven o'clock in the morning."

As I lay in bed I relived my sorry life. It was paved with excuses that I had made up for everybody who had hurt me. I rationalized everything. I told myself that Gary had not come because he was afraid of physicians and hospitals.

It was March 17th and promptly at eleven o'clock, Gary was there to pick us up, but he stayed downstairs in the lobby. He paid the bill and sent the suitcase upstairs and waited for us. The nurse tended to the baby while I dressed up. I was wheeled downstairs and finally, I had to face my husband. He blushed a little, shyly looked at me and asked how I was. He told me to wait there while he went to get the car. Not once did he look at or comment on the baby. The nurse was slightly bewildered but she said nothing.

On the way home, Gary talked about everything except the baby and me. He didn't mention that he had not come to see me or even ask how I had gotten to the hospital. I was sure he had inquired about that and gotten the information from the doctor. As we drove home Gary was very cautious. He drove very slowly. I caught him looking at the baby.

"Kevin is the baby's name." I said.

"Where did you get a name like that?" He asked.

"I asked you to help me pick a name and you said you didn't want anything to do with it. So Kevin is his name."

The baby must have sensed the tension between us because he was as good as gold.

We were home at last. Gary hadn't changed. He never helped with the chores nor did he ever hold his baby. He became more demanding especially if I was busy with the baby. His demands had to be met first. One week later he started going into his rages again because I had to finish making the baby's formula, and I didn't immediately sit on the couch with him to watch television. He carried on like a two year old who did not get his way. He was jealous of the baby. He would curse, bang into things, and yell that he was neglected. I just pretended not to hear him as I did my work in the kitchen.

I was shocked at what he did next. He barged into the kitchen completely nude. He was like a mad man. Sick as this may seem, I could not resist him. It had been a long time since we had made love. He started to hug me and I pushed him away. This only strengthened his resolve and made him more demanding. How he loved a challenge. He came toward me and said:

"Mel, just let me hold you and kiss you. I've been so lonesome without you."

He had me in his arms and started to kiss my neck and to caress me as he slowly began to take my clothes off. His mouth found mine and I was lost in the demands of passion. We made passionate love in the middle of the kitchen floor oblivious to anyone and everything else. We ended up in the shower and then on the bed. We were lying there basking in the moment. Kevin seemed to sense what was happening. He kept quiet the whole time.

A few moments later, the baby cried for his bottle. I got up and took a big chance. I cradled him and placed him on the bed in Gary's arms. I asked him to take care of him for a few moments while I prepared the baby's bottle. I didn't wait for an answer. I just walked out of the room. I peeked into the room and I saw the baby smiling and cooing at his daddy. Gary actually kissed his son on the forehead. I was so happy I could have cried. I knew that Gary loved his son. Once again I forgot about the hurtful things that had happened to me. We continued our usual routine of lovemaking. Gary knew I was weak and could not resist him.

Laurie came to visit me one afternoon with a present for the baby. She had her baby with her. He was named after her husband Jack. He was so cute. He looked a little like my Kevin. They were only two weeks apart and were about the same size.

I apologized for not having a gift for her. She told me not to worry. Her family had had a great baby shower for her and she absolutely didn't need a thing. We spent a lovely afternoon together. I really wanted to invite her and her husband to dinner but I knew that I would have to check with Gary first.

When Gary came home for dinner, I caught him smiling at the baby, and then he spotted the gift that Laurie had brought. His face was distorted and he spewed out accusations,

"Where did you get this? You can't fool me. It's from the baby's father. The minute I think I can trust you, you sneak behind my back. You are nothing but a whore."

The more I tried to explain who the donor was, the angrier he became. He was a mad man. He kicked me, hit me, and swore at me. The pain was excruciating. He left me on the floor as he went upstairs. I picked myself up, dressed the baby and readied myself to leave but I heard strange noises from upstairs. I went up and saw Gary sobbing. I resisted the temptation to console him, as I had done so many times in the past. I took the baby and left. I drove for hours and then realized that I had no place to go. I ached all over and I knew I was pregnant again. This made me nauseous.

9

As I drove home I was more and more convinced that Gary was a sick man and he needed help before he did something tragic. It wasn't normal for someone to be loving and sweet one moment and become mean and abusive the next moment. After all his rages, he would cry like a baby and tell me he was terribly sorry for his behavior. He told me he didn't remember half of the things he did during his rages. He said that he would get terrible pounding headaches and his mind would go blank.

I thought of all these things as I drove and I rationalized that going back home wouldn't be such a terrible ordeal. I would help Gary seek medical help and we would be happy. I knew Gary was certain that Kevin was his. The jealous accusations he made stemmed from the fact that he was ill. I was determined to get him help.

As I neared the house I grew anxious and nervous. I didn't know what to expect. I knew he wouldn't try to hit me again. The house was in total darkness. I shivered as I held onto Kevin tightly. I unlocked the door and turned on the lights. The house was a mess after Gary's little escapade. I put Kevin down and started cleaning. I heard a strange noise coming from the bathroom behind the kitchen. I went to investigate and I found Gary sitting on the toilet holding his wrist. The blood was gushing out. I screamed and he said:

"I'm sorry Mel, I thought you and the baby had left me."

"I've got to get you to the hospital, or you will bleed to death."

"No, No….."

I called the rescue squad and then called Laurie to come for Kevin. I covered for Gary and told the medical personnel that Gary had hurt himself with the butcher knife. I don't know if they believed me but nothing more was ever said.

Gary was out of danger. He seemed very pale but the doctor assured me he would be fine. I mentioned Gary's headaches to the doctor. I didn't go into any detail but I asked him if he could look for a cause because Gary got them very often. The doctor assured me he would check into it.

The following day the doctor asked Gary about his headaches. Gary replied:

"What headaches?'

"Your wife told me you get them quite often."

"She tends to exaggerate. I think that they are mostly tension headaches. I get them after a strenuous day. I have a tremendous amount of responsibility as a boss, you know." Gary replied.

Gary told me that the doctor had checked him out and had told him he was a nervous person, but otherwise he was in good health. Gary proceeded to tell me in no uncertain terms:

"I told you that I was in good shape. You think I'm crazy! Don't you ever get a shrink to check me out again or you won't live to tell about it."

I could tell that he was out of breath and exhausted, so I told him to rest. As I watched him sleep, I knew I could never leave him. Gary needed special tests to determine what his problem was. I promised myself that I would do my best to convince him to admit it.

Things were a little better at home. I could see that Gary was trying to control his temper. I told him we were going to have another baby. He wasn't very happy but he didn't say anything. The pills the doctor had given him for his tension headaches were helping. His only reaction to the news of my pregnancy was that I should remind him to stay away from him. That way I wouldn't make another brat. I was delighted by his remark. It only meant that he knew the baby was his. I was not unfaithful.

He surprised me one day when he brought home the most adorable puppy. He was a golden retriever. He told me that if I insisted on having all of these kids that we'd need a dog to protect them. I was really happy. He'd be a great companion for the kids and me. I loved animals and I think that Gary loved them even more. We named the dog Bosco and he became Gary's faithful companion.

Karen was dainty and so pretty. Our daughter was born nine and a half months after Kevin. Here I was alone again in the hospital. At least this time Gary had driven me to the hospital, kissed me, and said,

"Call me when you're ready to come home."

As I lay in the hospital bed staring at the lone rose that Gary had sent me, I wondered what life had in store for me. I knew I would have more children. Gary would not give up his wants or his ways of having sex for anybody or anything. The more I tried to resist him the more demanding and passionate he would get. I couldn't figure him out. I dozed off into a sound sleep. I woke up to the sound of the telephone. It was Gary.

"Hi, sweetheart, it's Gary."

"What's wrong Gary? Is something wrong with Kevin?"

"No, everything is fine. I went to my parent's after work to pick up Kevin and they insisted on keeping him until you come home from the hospital. I'm home now gathering a few things for them. Is that all right with you?"

Was I still dreaming? Was Gary asking for my approval? What a change! He must have swallowed the whole bottle of pills.

"Sweetheart, are you still there?" He continued.

"Yes, Gary, if Kevin is happy it's no problem. I don't want him to be afraid. I hope he's not too much trouble for your parents."

"Believe me, they have no problem with him and seem very happy. I miss you Mel. It's lonesome in this big house without you. The house is so empty it gives me the creeps. I could never live here without you. Hurry home you won't be sorry. I love you. Goodnight."

Was I talking to my husband? I wanted to freeze this moment in time. It was miraculous. Maybe Gary was changing. I prayed and hoped that the future would be good for us.

I dreamed about him that night. He was so handsome and I imagined that my life would be perfect now that we had a little girl who looked just like him.

A much friendlier Gary took us home from the hospital. He even looked at the baby and commented on how small she was. I assured him that she was fine and we would fatten her up quickly. His genuine concern thrilled me and gave me hope.

He kept looking at me all the way home and that convinced me he truly loved me in his own way. In my own way I reciprocated this love. Once we were home he held onto me tightly. For a long time we stayed locked in each other's arms. He then held me at arms' length and I noticed a small tear brushing his cheek. He cleared his throat and said:

"Hey, don't you want to see your little boy?"

He kissed me and went to get Kevin at his parents' house. I went into the house and was surprised at the neatness of the rooms. Gary had really done a good job. I started to prepare dinner. I was feeling well physically and emotionally. I was so excited when I heard the truck pull up in the driveway.

"Kevin, Kevin!" I cried out and gave him a hug.

He pulled away from me as though I were a stranger. He held onto his father. It didn't take him long to warm up to me when we got into the house. This little nine and half month boy was walking and getting into everything.

Life continued in the same humdrum way; however I was much busier. I had to keep a constant watch on Kevin and tend to Karen who was a fussy and demanding baby. This did not leave much time for Gary who was upset but managed to resign himself. He did manage to purposely tease me and I almost gave in to him once or twice.

He was playing games with me. Every night he would lie completely nude on the bed. I pretended not to notice. I went about the room ignoring him. One night he reached for me I did not resist the pull of his hands. My legs didn't hold me steadily so I collapsed against him. He put his arms around me and cuddled me. He held me and felt the lack of resistance in my body. He knew that he could do whatever he wanted with me. I shivered and my hands reached out to him.

"I don't want you to touch me." I said.

He didn't answer. He just pulled my sweater upward. My arms went up unresistingly with the movement. He slipped the sweater over my head and messed up my hair. My seeming lack of interest only made him more persistent.

"I don't want to make love to you now."

Those words only succeeded in turning him on. He said, "Lie down."

Obediently, I stretched out on the bed. Once again I was a slave to his passion. Gary had won. He put me through such ecstasy. I was as over passionate as he was. Even after a beating I couldn't resist him. I had such a depraved craving inside of me. I needed to love and to be loved. We were both exhausted after our session.

Gary looked at me and smiled. My arms went around him and we kissed for the first time that night. I couldn't resist him. I truly loved him and I so wanted to love him and be loved by him. He whispered,

"You make me crazy. How I love to make love to you."

"Yes, we're so good together."

It was a difficult year. I was expecting my third child. It was a much harder pregnancy than the other two. I managed to continue with my chores, but I was exhausted.

10

My mother passed away two years after my father died. I was saddened by the fact that I had not been able to be close to her. I also felt that I could have done more to brighten her miserable life. I guess hindsight is always twenty twenty.

It was a very small funeral. Mother did not have many friends. She kept to herself most of the time. It was both good and uncomfortable to meet with my brothers. We didn't really know each other. My sister Nancy made me promise to call her. She lived only two hours away.

My siblings proceeded to tell me about the wonderful lives they were leading and they couldn't wait to hear about my life with Gary. My brothers had never visited me because they disliked Gary immensely. I told them that he was a wonderful husband, provider and father to his children. Gary had been unable to come to the funeral because he had to care for the children. They didn't say anything but I could see by the expressions on their faces that they didn't believe me. We said goodbye and I prepared for my flight back.

On my way home I thought about how my life was nothing but a lie. Gary had done everything in his power to prevent me from going to the funeral. As he threatened and ranted about what he would do to me if I dared go to the funeral, his parents stopped for a visit. He knew he couldn't let his father see his outrageous behavior. He had to act like the devoted father and husband they thought he was. I took advantage of their visit and I mentioned the death of my mother and my plans to attend the funeral.

Irene was not aware that my mother had moved to Florida after the death of my father. She was living with my two brothers. They chose to bury her in their new town and they were paying for all the expenses.

"Oh, so you'll have to fly to Florida as soon as possible." Irene said.

"That's impossible!" Gary shouted.

Then he lowered his voice and added that I had too many responsibilities at home.

"Now Gary, we have to work something out." His mother replied.

"She wasn't close..."

"I don't want to hear another word." Interrupted Irene.

I really believe she knew more than she let on but she was going to be discreet. Irene offered to pay for my flight and offered to stay with her grandchildren.

"No way," Gary replied," that's asking too much. I don't need your money, I have plenty of my own."

"It's settled, son", Gary's father interrupted, "since you have enough money, you pay for the trip and we'll baby-sit the children. I'll hear no more about it. Let's go home dear."

Gary was stunned as he watched his parents leave. He then turned and slapped me in the face and yelled:

"You conniving son of a bitch. How dare you use my parents to get what you want?"

I could tell he wanted to hurt me and even kill me. That evening he put me through a tortuous hell, physically and sexually.

"That's what you get for defying me, for sneaking behind my back and for disobeying me."

My 'master' had spoken. How I hated him for degrading me so. He had absolutely no respect for me.

I was having second thoughts about going to the funeral. Was it worth all the trouble, humiliation, accusations and beatings I would incur because of this trip? I almost decided to stay home but then I told myself I would have to suffer all of these things anyhow. I decided to take the trip. I wished that I had made more of an effort to visit my mother even if she had said that she didn't want to ever see me again. I was almost happy and giddy to take my first flight - my first trip away from Gary, until I realized the reason for the trip. I thought of the possibility of not retuning. I knew and Gary knew I could never leave because of the children. I came back home.

Thank God that I had told Gary of my pregnancy before I left. He would have a fit if he found out after my return. He'd accuse me of being unfaithful and oversexed. If he really believed everything that he said, he would have killed me. Instead, he used his filthy accusations to fuel his sexual desire and rage.

He put me through three hours of exhausting lovemaking. This was my punishment. I don't know how he made it to work the next day.

I gave birth to my third child, Kathleen. Gary played the same role as he had before. He took me to the hospital, didn't visit, and sent me the lone long stemmed rose. At home he was very indifferent. He kept to himself lost in deep thought. Once in a while, he played with the children and his dog. He even offered to take us for a rare ride in his car.

11

Three months after Kathy was born, Gary came home and announced that he had bought a hardware store. I couldn't imagine why. He was so excited.

"Does that mean you're going to quit your job?" I asked him.

"Of course not. I'm going to run the store on a part time basis. I'll open it two or three nights a week and on Saturdays."

I wasn't going to bother to object to this idea because what Gary wanted Gary got. I tried to put a positive spin on this subject and I told myself it would give him the opportunity to be away from the children. I knew he loved them but I also knew that they made him very nervous. I figured he'd be more pleasant when he was home if he were away for longer periods.

Gary never volunteered any information about the store. It's a good thing I didn't have a jealous nature. Whenever I asked him how things were, he assured me that I didn't have to worry. Everything was fine. I never doubted his fidelity. He wouldn't have been so passionate every night if he had been seeing other women.

My days were filled with all kinds of activities. Laurie and I had become close friends. Gary's mood swings had improved but we lacked the closeness we had once shared. Gary lived in his own world and had his own ideas. He included me only when he wanted sex. He had not cultivated any new friendships. He was considered to be a nice, shy, and quiet guy. He received many invitations for outings but he refused them. Everyone accepted him the way he was.

He avoided the neighbors and did not like visitors. In fact if people came to the house they didn't stay very long. They were most uncomfortable with Gary. He never went out of his way to make them feel welcomed. Once in a great while he would visit his parents. I was very lonely and feeling depressed.

I felt I just had to talk to someone or go insane. I gathered all my strength and approached Gary. I couldn't hold back the tears and I was sobbing uncontrollably. Gary came into the bedroom. To my amazement he put his arms around me and held me as he would have held a small child.

"I know I know sweetheart. I'm no good for you. You deserve much better. I don't know what is wrong with me. I keep telling myself that I have to change and every time I try, something happens inside of me. I want to show my love and it only turns into savageness and hatred. My insides are in a constant turmoil. I shiver and all the love I want to show you and the children just doesn't come out that way. I have dreams where my arms are extended to you and the children. Try as I might, I can't reach you. You seem to be running away and you disappear. I wake up in a cold sweat, feeling so empty and alone. I just can't figure it out."

I was so touched with this moment of honesty. I put my arms around him and softly said:

"Darling, let me help you."

Wrong thing to say! Gary stiffened. Realizing that he had divulged his inner feelings, his macho pride took over and he quickly changed attitude.

"What the hell makes you think I need help? You're the one who needs help. You're always getting pregnant, giving me more responsibilities than I can handle, You know that kids make me nervous, yet you flaunt your sexy body in front of me until I can't resist you."

I was so outraged. I didn't let him finish. I shouted:

"You call yourself a man? You have the nerve to stand there and blame me for getting pregnant. When we were supposed to abstain because it wasn't a safe period, you only became more demanding. One week after the baby was born you insisted on making love. I know that I should have resisted, but YOU are just as responsible as I am. We both are to blame. If you do not want to have any more children STAY away from me unless you have protection. That's an order."

He slapped me and told me I had no right to tell him how and when to have sex. He then smacked me across the mouth.

"I've had it with you. You don't really care about me or the children." I said. "I can't take any more of your moods and abuse. By tomorrow, the children and I will be out your life forever. I don't know what we'll do yet, but we'll manage."

I was so caught up in telling Gary off, I hadn't noticed that he was clutching his head. His body was shaking jerkily. I froze. I don't remember anything beyond that point. I must have passed out because when I came to, I was lying on the floor. I was completely nude. I was in the corner of the bedroom and I couldn't move. My mouth was swollen and my whole body was bruised. I couldn't even cry out. I was in so much pain. I wanted to just fall asleep and never wake up again. I tried to scream but only a whimper came out. I thought that I would die of fright. Gary had a basin filled with warm water. He also had a towel and a bag of ice.

"What a great doctor. He's looking out for his patient." I thought sarcastically.

He picked me up and gently put me on the bed. He washed the blood off carefully. I noticed he had tears in his eyes. This time I did not show any kind of tenderness or forgiveness. I only had feelings of pain, humiliation, and hatred. Gary finally got me into my nightgown and gave me two pills for the pain. I just wanted to lie there and die, but I knew that I had to get better for my children.

Gary slept in the other room but throughout the night I could feel his presence in the room. I pretended to be sleeping. The following day Gary took the day out of work. He came into the room with a breakfast tray and kissed me on the forehead. He told me to rest and not to worry about anything. He had everything under control.

I didn't answer. I just kept praying for guidance and strength. Everything seemed so hopeless. When I had previously told Gary that I was going to leave, I was going to call my sister and ask her if she could take us in until I figured out what I could do. I would swallow my pride and tell her everything and I knew that she would do something for me.

Downstairs everything seemed to be calm. Gary was taking care of the children. He seemed to have calmed down and did not lose his temper. I'm sure they were puzzled. They were so young, but they had to be aware of the situation. They weren't always asleep when he had his flare-ups. They had witnessed more than one of his escapades. I really felt horrible and sickened. They seemed to be resilient. They went about playing and enjoying themselves.

After Gary had put the children to bed he came into the bedroom. I thought he was going to apologize but all he said was that he had made arrangements to stay home for the week. Then he added with tears in his eyes:

"I hope I didn't hurt our baby. I really do love you and our children."

Then he tiptoed out of the room.

The following week was one of the best weeks I had ever spent with my family and with Gary. It was regretful that it had to be preceded by the worst nightmare of my life. Gary cooked, cleaned, whistled and played with the children. He even took us out. We went to a drive-in movie and one day we went on a picnic. Gary tried to be even tempered but I could see he was becoming tense and nervous. How I prayed that he would consult a doctor. I was not brave enough to broach the subject again. Talking about it would only precipitate another beating.

12

I decided to talk to his mother. I didn't know how to question her tactfully, so I nonchalantly questioned her about Gary's childhood. She seemed nervous and wanted to avoid the questions. She told me that Gary had been a normal child and I could tell she loved him very much. She said:

"I was worried he wouldn't be normal because I was forty-eight when I carried him. I had him checked periodically and the doctors were amazed by his progress. He was ahead of children his own age both physically and mentally. I did spoil Gary. He was the miracle child I thought I would never have. Once in a while, if he didn't have his own way he would fake a headache and go into a tantrum. He was a loner. He used to spend hours taking things apart and putting them together again. He was used to having things his own way and he didn't like to share. He was so smart in school that he skipped a grade. A few years later the teachers wanted him to skip another grade but I wouldn't allow it. Why are you asking me all of these things, Melanie? Are you having any problems?"

"Me? No, I just wanted to know if there was something in his past that brought on his frequent headaches and the rages they bring on."

I must have touched a nerve because I saw another Irene. My mother-in-law who had always been gentle and courteous replied tersely,

"It's no wonder that Gary has so many headaches with all the responsibilities you've straddled him with. You've been selfish and demanding. You've tricked my Gary into having all of these children when you know he is high strung and nervous. You knew he didn't want any children. Now, you have the nerve to suggest that he is not normal. Why are you trying to blame his behavior on something from his past? The fault is yours. You're the one who is not normal. Try to control your sexual appetite and think of the consequences. I suggest that you get your tubes tied and then maybe Gary can relax and be himself again."

I couldn't believe her. I burst into tears and ran out of the house. I thought that my visit with Irene would help me clarify things but it only bewildered and confused me more. I should have known from experience that I was always alone. There never was anyone to help or console me.

The strangest thing about this whole episode was that I started to believe what she had said. I probably was the guilty party. Part of me wanted to believe this but the more rational part of me didn't accept her evaluation. I remembered that when we were single Gary had strange savage tendencies. I certainly was not responsible for those. He told me I was not like other woman and I brought out his passion to heights he had never known were possible. The thought of my being with any other man enraged him and made him want to kill me. I believed him. I considered his comments as a compliment. What did I know? I had never been with anyone else. Gary had taught me how to make love. I began to think I was the sick one and that I should seek help to control my insatiable passionate desires; however, the thought of having to confide in someone else terrified me. I decided to work it out myself. I would not tease Gary and I would stay out of his way.

I kept thinking that it was probably wrong for us to share such wild sexual intimacies. When Gary was in this state he became a maniac. He became so possessive and jealous and paranoid. I was so confused. I didn't know what to do, but I would try to control myself. Definitely the fault was mine.

As time went by, Gary really tried to be good. Since the beating incident he rarely came near me. It was easier for me to curb my desires. I still yearned for him and I could tell that he did too. I was pregnant and it would have been a 'safe' time.

On February twelve, I gave birth to our son Kenneth. I had two boys and two girls-a perfect family. Gary had driven me to the hospital and sent me my one rose. His parents came to visit me and brought me a box of chocolates. I was embarrassed at the sight of my mother-in-law. She sensed this and she came over kissed me and whispered:

"I'm sorry for everything I said to you. I didn't mean any of it. Please, forgive me."

Nothing more was ever said. My in-laws stayed with the children while I was in the hospital. They did not know that Gary never came to see me. I never told them.

Gary's parents offered to keep the children with them until I was fully recovered. It was a great help to me. It took me longer to recover and I think that Gary noticed it because he was particularly attentive and helpful. That week we were very close in spite of the fact that we didn't have sex. I really missed the children and I insisted that Gary go get them. He told me I wasn't strong enough yet. Finally I said to him:

"Don't you think your parents have had them long enough? They are probably all worn out. They aren't young any more."

"Yeah, yeah, I'll go get them." He replied.

I was so happy when they came home. Once again we would be a family.

13

It was springtime again, my favorite time of the year. We now called our home a farm because of the animals and the land. It was so peaceful. The pansies were coming up and the fragrance of the lilac trees was delightful. We had worked so hard on the landscaping. The young buds on the trees made me aware of new beginnings and gave me hope. Flowering trees and bushes graced our home. Gary and I enjoyed working together and we had succeeded in making our home look like a beautiful pastoral painting. We had taken pictures of the magnificent sunrises and sunsets. It was well worth all of the time, effort, and love that we had put into working and making our home a little slice of paradise. We absolutely loved it.

We didn't have too many animals. We had mostly cats, rabbits, and chickens. Springtime was a great time for the children to witness new births and appreciate the wonders of nature. They loved to play with the animals and romp in the fields. It was a carefree time for them and for me. Karen loved to tend to the newborn animals. She loved to pet them and feed them. She and the other children had names for them. They sometimes dressed them and tried to teach them tricks. It was wonderful to see them 'enjoying' themselves.

Gary had built a barn, a shed, and the fencing. Originally the property, was only rocks and ledge. We had certainly transformed it. I often caught sights of Gary walking around the yard. He gazed at his handy work with approval and pride.

These glimpses assured me that there was a tender, sensitive man buried inside of Gary. My problem was to figure out how to reach him.

We also had worked on the inside of the house. Our favorite room was the huge front room where the main attraction was the field stone fireplace. Directly in front of the fireplace was a large plush couch where we spent many hours. It was our romantic getaway. On a cool night we would enjoy the warmth of the fire reading good books. We were avid readers and spent many nights in this little haven where we were lost in the world of make believe. On the other wall there was a library with bookcases that Gary had built. On his good days Gary was very creative and handy. He could tackle any project and do it brilliantly.

I wondered what the remainder of the year held in store for me. I hoped and prayed that it would be good.

"Please God, watch over me and the kids. Help Gary find help for whatever problem he has."

14

Gary tried very hard to be good and for the most part he succeeded. He kept himself busy. I noticed that when he started to have a strange look in his eyes, a sign of an impending headache, he would go out to his truck. He would return looking so sad and depressed. The worst part of all this was that we both knew what was going on but I didn't dare discuss it with him. I had learned my lesson and I never mentioned anything nor did I suggest the need for professional help.

I was proud of myself. I had curbed my sexual appetite and kept my promise. It was difficult because Gary was being so pleasant. We just tried to avoid each other but one night, I went through a difficult test. Gary came home with four roses. He gave them to me and told me that they were for the mother of his four children. It did not take much more than that to make me forget all of the abuse I had endured. I was not fearful but hopeful.

"Surely, Gary was better."

A moment of sanity came back to me and I told myself to be careful or I would be disappointed. It was a good thing that he couldn't read my thoughts. I put my arms around him and kissed him tenderly. I could feel the passion mounting and I held him at arms' length and stared into his deep blue eyes. He reciprocated by whispering sweet nothings that I longed to hear. He knew just what I wanted to hear. He told me that

I was a terrific kisser. He continued to kiss me and caress me until I was ready to succumb to his demands but I managed to whisper:

"Gary, it's not a safe time."

He groaned and I was ready to throw caution to the wind. To my surprise he pulled away. He went to get himself a glass of water. He sat by the sink and just looked at me adoringly. I went to him and tried to bring back the mood that we had just experienced. He stepped back and said:

"Please Mel. You said that it was not safe."

He went into the bathroom and prepared himself for bed.

15

Our social life was literally non-existent. We had so much work to do around the house. The four children took up much of our time. I was so tired that I would be in bed by the time Gary came from work.

The children were all healthy. Kevin, our oldest, was such a joy. He was just like his father without the rage and temper. He was an intelligent, creative, hardworking child. He adored his father and I thought the feeling was mutual. Gary would find things for him to do. Once in a while on Saturdays he would take him to the store with him. I would then go to pick him up. I didn't want Gary to overdo it. One day, I was astonished and pleased when I got to the store. Gary had a work area all set up for Kevin. There was woodworking material and all that he needed for his projects. Gary was so proud as he bragged about his son. He said:

"Come and see some of things he built on his own. He is so creative and hardworking."

He continued to rave about his son's accomplishments. I was glad there was no one in the store. I would have been embarrassed.

Karen was a much more serious child. She was like a little old lady. She worried about everything. She tried to mother the other two children. She was always trying to help and finding chores to do. I worried about her. I thought she was missing out on her childhood. She followed me around as though she wanted to protect me from harm. She was lovable and I made sure that she was loved. I remembered my childhood and I swore that my children would never lack for affection.

Kathleen was as mischievous as she was beautiful. She didn't have a care in the world. She was like a butterfly flitting about touching everything. She loved to tattle on her siblings. She had such a way about her that it was difficult to get angry with her. She was not afraid of Gary and she would crawl up on his lap and shower him with kisses and hugs. He didn't seem to mind. When he was tired, he gently put her down and left the room. She was like Karen in some ways. She was very sensitive and pensive.

Kenny had light brown curly hair and brown eyes like mine. He was a perfect, happy boy. He also loved his father and he always tried to imitate Kevin.

I mustn't forget Bosco, our beloved dog. He loved all of us but he was Gary's best friend. He seemed to sense his moods and adapted his responses to him. He brought so much joy to the whole family. He played and pretended to be our protector. His bark was bigger than his bite. I suppose he would have protected us if we had been in danger. Who knows?

Didn't I just describe the perfect family? Unfortunately, events would prove that it wasn't so perfect.

16

One day Gary came home from work and announced that he had joined a bowling league with the boys from work. He was always full of surprises. I didn't think he even knew how to bowl. I didn't dare say anything negative. I told him it was a good idea. Once again I had a glimmer of hope. He was actually going to make an effort to be sociable for the first time in his life.

Maybe he was getting better. He didn't seem to be having his headaches anymore. He wasn't losing his temper so often. Then again I hardly ever saw him. He was always at work or at the store. I figured it was better that way. The children were more relaxed.

I became friendlier with Laurie because I had fewer problems at home. I was not afraid to spend more time with her. I avoided her when I had violent episodes with Gary. I felt like a new woman and I enjoyed cultivating my friendship with Laurie. We spent more time together during the week. We would take the kids to the park or take them shopping. Sometimes we just enjoyed each other's company over coffee. I hadn't yet told her about my problems with Gary. She kept asking Gary and me to come to her house to play cards on Saturday nights. I told her that Gary was the shy type and that he did not like to socialize. She was smart enough not to press any further.

Laurie taught me how to crochet and knit. She wanted me to join her friend's Wednesday night club. Every week they would meet at someone's house to knit and socialize. Every week they had the meeting at someone else's house. Laurie told me that I wouldn't have it at my house. She would have the get-together at hers when it was my turn.

"I really don't mind. I love to entertain." She said

I envied her. She seemed to have such a nice life without tension or pressure. She could do anything she wanted to and her husband was always in agreement. Laurie didn't seem to take advantage of her husband's goodness. She was a good mother and housewife. Her house and children were always spotless. She made sure that she always got home in time to prepare a good meal for her family. I did all of those things for my family but I couldn't do what I wanted. It just wasn't fair, but I knew there wasn't anything I could do about it.

I really wanted to join the knitting club but the more I thought about it the more I knew Gary would not approve. He was too jealous and too suspicious. I had never asked him to baby-sit. I really wanted this night out. I told him flat out that I was joining. I didn't ask him. He wasn't crazy about the idea but he didn't say anything. I forgot to tell him it would be at a different house each week. He thought that I would be at Laurie's every week. I would soon find out *that* was a mistake.

It was great to be with women my own age. I noticed that no one had a husband like mine. They talked about their social lives and all of the things they did as families. I didn't even have a social life. The only thing that Gary and I had in common was our sexual life. I wasn't about to share any of these details, although they were pretty open about theirs. I am sure they exaggerated but it was fun to hear. I really enjoyed my night out. It made the rest of week more bearable.

I met one of my neighbors Mary who lived down the street. I liked her and we became friends. I would have her visit me once in a while during the day.

On Tuesday nights, Gary's bowling nights, I made sure his meal was ready and his clothes were laid out on the bed. I wanted to be sure he had time to relax before he left. It was not the same story on Wednesday nights. He would purposely come home late and take his time eating. He wanted to be sure I would be late washing the dishes, bathing the children, and getting ready. He didn't cooperate at all. In fact he would make it harder for me every week. One week I had had it. He came in late for supper. I hadn't waited for him. The children were fed and ready for bed and the dishes were done. The look on his face was enough to kill me.

"Where's my supper?" He demanded.

"In the oven. Get it yourself. I am busy with the children." I replied.

He grabbed me by the hair and pulled me into the kitchen. He flung me toward the stove. I hit the door with my side. I was doubled over with pain. He then kicked me in the rump and demanded his meal. He said:

"Well things are going to change around here. You've been getting away with too much lately. You think you can just go off and do as you please. Well think again."

As he was yelling at me he had me by the roots of my hair and he bent me backwards. How he enjoyed to hurt me and to make me beg! He made me tell him how sorry I was; how I wouldn't disobey him any more; and how much I loved him. He had me repeat degrading sexual things. He forced me to say I didn't really want to go out that night; I wanted to stay home and be his sex slave. He was pathetic. He got pleasure out of seeing me cry and beg. He finally released me when I told him I had to call Laurie and tell her I wouldn't be going with her. Gary had a smirk on his face. He had won.

I avoided Laurie the next day. I was so depressed. The children must have sensed something was wrong because they were exceptionally good. Karen my little mother figure had taken over. She was taking care of the younger ones. When Gary came home at night he acted as though everything was normal. It was so bizarre to see this madman take on the role of an angel.

"What a hypocrite!" I thought. "Where is his conscience – his sense of decency?"

"Let's hurry with supper kids." He said. "I'll take you all out for ice cream. I'm sure Bosco wants some too."

The children were wild with excitement. What a role Gary played. He could have won an academy award. The previous night he was beating up their mother and today he was a gentle loving father so dedicated to the welfare and pleasure of his children. How I wished that I could have told them. I swallowed hard and forced a smile.

After supper, he helped me with the dishes. He was trying to be affectionate but he sensed my apathy. He kept his distance because of the children. I was fearful because I knew from past experiences that my indifference turned him on.

'Let's hop into the car." He shouted gleefully.

I remembered that it was Thursday night.

"What about the shop? Tonight is Thursday and you always work on Thursday nights." I said.

"So, the hell with it. I'll either open a little later, or depending on..."

He started rubbing my back.

"I won't open at all."

"Gary, I don't feel like going for ice cream. Why don't you just enjoy the kids and the dog? Go without me." I replied.

"Mel, you're coming. If you don't come, nobody is going. I'll have the kids get out of the car."

So I went, he didn't go to the shop and we made love all night. How sad!

Gary continued to make it difficult for me on Wednesday nights. I didn't let his attitude discourage me. There was no way I was going to give up my little breath of fresh air.

Nothing seemed to ever go smoothly for a long period of time in my life. One Wednesday evening after the club meeting Laurie dropped me off at my house as she usually did. That night the meeting had been held at Jeanne's house. I was happy as I walked into the house. I was greeted by a slap in the face. I knew from experience how to react. I stayed down and pretended to be really hurt. I stayed there until he calmed down. He then got down on his knees and started stroking my head. He said:

"Why did you do it Mel? Why did you lie to me? I was just starting to trust you again. Why? You know that I can't bear to think of you with another man. Now I'm going to have to kill you."

He was serious. I was terrified and I couldn't move. I was afraid of dying and I believed that he'd rather kill me than have me leave or be unfaithful. I knew just how to handle him before he lost control. I resorted to the same sick tactics that had worked previously.

Gary was jealous, over possessive, and paranoid. His latest rage was also fueled by his lack of information. This was partially my fault. I hadn't told him the meetings were held at a different house each week. I didn't want to have to explain why they were never held at my house. He would never have allowed it.

That evening, Kenney woke up crying. Gary thought he had a fever so he called Laurie's house to speak to me and ask me what to do. Jack, Laurie's husband answered and told Gary that the girls were meeting at Jeanne's that week. I could just imagine what was going through Gary's sick mind.

"That's what you think, brother." Gary said as he abruptly hung up the phone.

Jack was puzzled and concerned. He couldn't wait to tell Laurie. The next day Laurie told me she worried all night. When she saw me she could see I had been beaten up pretty badly. I said it was my fault. I should have told him we went to different houses every week. I told her he was extremely jealous and possessive and when he found out that I was not where he thought I was, he was furious.

"So you see, Laurie, I was at fault." I said.

" How often does this happen?" She asked.

"Oh, not too often." I lied. "He was so worried about the baby. He was out of his mind and he lost his temper."

Laurie sensed that I was protecting my husband and she didn't press me any further. She didn't want to embarrass me.

Later during the week when Gary seemed to be relatively calm, I explained the whole situation to him. I even apologized for not having been honest with him from the very beginning. I don't know if he believed me or not. Once again he won. I gave up my Wednesday night outings.

I stayed home and didn't go anywhere. He would check on me constantly. He'd come home unexpectedly at night and ask the children if anybody had come to see me or if I had gone anywhere.

17

I only wanted four children, but I was pregnant again. I didn't know how I was going to tell Gary. He believed I had a boyfriend. I put off telling him about it. Christmas was just around the corner and Gary was unusually good humored. He came home one day with the most gorgeous Christmas tree. The children were so excited. I tried to calm them down because I was afraid Gary would get nervous. To my amazement Gary joined in with them. I didn't want to take any chances so I decided to give each one of them a chore to do. I sensed that the children knew why I was acting this way. They had witnessed many of their father's mood swings. There was no back talk. They immediately got busy. God knows how they feared Gary when he was in one of his bad moods.

It was a great fun night. After supper Gary helped me clean up. We lit a fire in the fireplace and got out all the decorations. The children couldn't have been better behaved. They waited anxiously to be invited to help. Gary was uncharacteristically pleasant. He called to them and said:

"Come on kids, let's get this tree decorated."

The memory of this night is forever etched in my mind. It was the best! Gary and the children were beaming with joy as they busied themselves around the tree. There was so much warmth in that room that night emanating from the fireplace, the pine smell, the smile on Gary's face, and the happiness of my children. Gary even picked up the little one so that he could put tinsel on the top branches. What a scene to be treasured.

I picked up the stool and brought it to the tree. I wanted to stand on it and straighten the star. Gary quickly put his hands around my waist and carried me off. He said,

"I don't think you should be stretching like that, especially in your condition. You wouldn't want to hurt our baby would you?"

My heart stopped beating. I looked at him bewildered.

"Well, after four kids, don't you think I recognize the signs?" He said softly.

"Please dear God. Don't let anything spoil this evening."

I was so afraid that everything would change as it always had in the past.

"Next time, don't be afraid to tell me."

"Next time." I replied. "I hope there is no next time."

"Well, with our luck, I wouldn't count on it."

He put his arms around me and whispered:

"I think I married a baby making machine." He laughed. "Then again, we sure make damn nice kids don't we, Mrs. D.?"

My husband was truly a Doctor Jekyll and Mr. Hyde. I was happy for the evening and I was going to enjoy it.

"Well, kids, I hate to do this but it's way past your bed time."

I got them ready for bed and just before they went to their rooms, they tiptoed to their father kissed him and thanked him for being in a good mood and letting them have fun with him. I was so worried that Gary would go into a rage over the remark about the 'good' mood. He surprised me and he held them in his arms for a moment and said,

"You're welcome kids. Sleep tight."

This was the man I had fallen in love with. I kissed him but I didn't know what to say to him. I did not want to break the spell by saying the wrong thing. This was a constant in our lives. I left many things unsaid because of his moods. This saddened me. I had to be on my guard all the time. The saddest part of all this was that I could not confide in him.

18

He was still in a good mood so I kissed him and we made love in front of the perfect fire. Gary could take me to a world of ecstasy that I had never dreamed existed. When he was good, he was perfect. When he was bad, he was pure evil.

Much to my amazement the good days and good moods continued. Gary took the kids and me Christmas shopping. Once in a while I'd see that strange look on his face. He was trying so hard to be in control. I would immediately take charge and try to make things easier for him, but we never talked about it. I wanted to talk to him, but I knew it was impossible. Whenever I brought up the subject he would go crazy.

We still had some shopping to do I knew that too much of the children's presence might cause Gary to lose his cool, so I suggested we get a baby-sitter and we could finish the shopping.

"I know a reliable person who lives across the street. Her name is Mary. We can't let the children see us buying presents. They still believe in Santa Claus."

Gary seemed a little angry. I started to blame myself for not phrasing it differently. Finally he calmed down and said:

"I was going to suggest we go without the children. I was going to ask my mother if she would take them, but a baby-sitter closer to home might be better. I have to check her out before I give my permission."

I had escaped his wrath, thank God. I agreed with him and made him think it was his idea and it was a great one. Having a baby-sitter was a novelty for the children and they loved the idea. When Gary saw how excited they were, he sat them down and read them the rules. He told them of the consequences they would face if they didn't behave. I was sure they would be good. They were too afraid of their father.

What a great time we had shopping. We even stopped for a snack. We did all of our shopping for the children and for his mother and father. We even bought Christmas stockings for each child to put above the fireplace. Gary told me that if the babysitter trial worked out well, then maybe we would go out again to buy some stocking stuffers, and probably go to a movie some Saturday night.

I was so happy but I didn't dare overreact. I was totally aware of his sick responses when I got too excited. Whenever I was excited or very happy about something it seemed to trigger in him the desire to hurt me. So I remained cool, and continued to talk about the children, the house, his parents, and our future. Not once did I mention our problem, his job, or his feelings about anything. He kept staring at me and he was actually embarrassing me. Finally he broke the spell and pulled me out the door towards the car.

"I love you so much Melanie. Let's make love right now."

"I want to. You're something else! Did you forget we are in a parking lot? We could get arrested."

He laughed, and said:

"Great headlines: *READ ALL ABOUT IT.* . . . 'Very pregnant woman arrested for making love to loving husband.'"

We drove away. He had one hand around me and I had mine on his groin and succeeded in getting him all worked up.

"You little witch, do you want me to have an accident?"

"I'm sorry," I said as I pulled my hand away.

"Don't stop, I'll be careful."

He kissed my forehead and we drove home. On our way, Gary took a detour on a deserted road.

"It's only nine thirty. It's too early to go home just yet. We don't want the baby-sitter to think we don't trust her do we?"

I knew what he had in mind and I was as eager as he was. I felt like a teenager. As we were preparing to make love the windows got so fogged up we couldn't see outside. I panicked and said,

"Gary, did you lock the door?"

"That's a hell of thing to think of at a moment like this."

I lost all sense of reality and succumbed to my desires and his demands. Finally we realized where we were and what we were doing. Gary said:

"Wow! We'll have to do it again."

I felt a tinge of remorse. Here we were two mature adults making love in the middle of winter in the nude, in a parked car, and I enjoyed it.

After we were dressed and ready to go home Gary told me he loved me. He then thanked me as he kissed me tenderly on the cheek.

Everything was fine at home. The baby-sitter had no complaints and the children were sleeping. Gary paid her and took her home. While he was gone I went to shower. I didn't hear Gary come back. He jumped into the shower and he was ready for another session. I was no better than he was. We started making love in the bathroom and we continued in the bedroom until we were exhausted and fell asleep. I hoped the children hadn't heard us.

The following day, Laurie came over for coffee,

"My! What happened to you? You're radiant." She asked.

"Nothing, we just had a fabulous time shopping. We accomplished a lot."

"Is that all it takes to make you happy?

Laurie knew there was more going on in my life. I didn't discuss it with her or anybody else. She never questioned me.

We were having coffee when the doorbell rang and Mary came in. She had coffee with us and then asked me if I wanted to join the clubhouse membership at the beach. She had already told me about the good times they had down there. The membership included parties for the children, dances for adults and participation in a private beach and playground activities. She continued and told me about the other benefits. I wanted to join but I was afraid of Gary's reaction. Mary sensed my dilemma and said,

"Mel, why don't you talk to Gary about the dance next Saturday night. You don't have to be a member to attend. If Gary enjoys himself, maybe he'll decide to join on his own. Please give it a try Mel, we'd love to have you go with us.

19

I talked to him about the club. I told him how inexpensive it was and that the membership included rights to the beach, the tennis courts and the playground. I asked him if we could join as soon as possible. Then the children could attend the Christmas party. I kept going on and on about all the perks and advantages there would be. He interrupted me by saying:

"Okay, slow down. I can see you're really enthusiastic. I'm not saying 'no' Mel, but I need some time to think about it."

"Thank you, thank you!" I said as I kissed him. "How about the dance on Saturday night? Would you take me? We don't have to stay the whole night if you're not enjoying yourself. We could probably go with Mary and her husband. You like them."

"Gee, I don't know —a dance. What the hell would I do at a dance? You know I don't like dances. Don't you remember?"

I suddenly remembered our first date and was almost sorry that I had suggested it. Gary sensed my disappointment and he said:

"I can see that you're hurt and I don't like to see you that way. So I'll tell you what. Seeing that I am such a nice guy, no smart remarks from you, young lady..." He added as he laughed. "As I was saying, the nice guy that I am says that we'll go."

I started jumping up and down like a little kid in a candy store.

"Calm down, I haven't finished. I said we would go but we will leave whenever I want to. Deal?"

I tried to restrain myself when I told him it was a 'deal'.

"When we leave the dance we are going to get into our car and find that detour on the dirt road. Do you know what I mean?"

I certainly knew what he meant. He started to tickle me and I laughed and screamed as we fell to the floor. The children heard us and I could see that they were afraid that they would witness another violent scene. I quickly said,

"Mommy and daddy are playing. Come on kids. Let's beat up daddy."

They jumped on us and we had a great time.

I couldn't wait to tell Mary we were going to the dance. She was both happy and surprised. She said we'd have a great time. No one was happier and excited than I was at that moment. Mary asked me what I was going to wear.

"Oh, my God, I had never given it a thought. Does it have to be something formal?"

"No," she replied, "it's very informal. It's a small clubhouse. You can wear anything that is comfortable. The people are very nice. Nobody looks down on anybody else. You and your husband are just like the rest of us. Don't worry about anything. I have to go now. Do you need anything at the store?"

"No thank you. Thanks for coming over." I replied.

I had a wonderful week. I tried to be more positive and not believe that when things went well something evil was about to happen. I was really trying to change my negative outlook on life. Things *would* be great, Gary *would* take me to the dance and we *would* have a fabulous time.

20

I was right. We made it to the dance. In fact, we even went
shopping the night before to get ready for the big night.
I arranged to meet Mary at the clubhouse. I didn't want
to do anything to aggravate Gary. As we were getting ready,
I noticed that Gary was very nervous. I wondered if we were
doing the right thing. I knew how rude he could be. I also
knew how he hated dances and social gatherings. I was about
to tell Gary I had changed my mind. Then I thought of my
newfound positive attitude. So I playfully asked,

"How do I look?

He answered nervously,

"Very, very pretty. Mel, please stay close to me all night.
Don't you dare dance with anyone else."

"I don't want to dance with anyone else. You are the
only man I love. You are all the man that I can handle." I
answered.

"Are you complaining, Mrs. D.?"

"Not at all, Mr. D. By the way, you look very handsome.
I'll have to keep my eye on you to make sure that nobody takes
you away." I replied.

We had arrived and I don't know who was more nervous.
We finally made our way to the hall and were greeted by Mary.
I'm sure she knew much more than I had ever told her. She
greeted us at the door, led us to our table, and introduced us to
everyone. Gary shook hands but offered little conversation.

"Glad that's over with. Can we go parking now?" He said
to me.

I turned to look at him and realized he was just teasing me.

The band was very good and we had started to join in the conversation. Gary was holding my hand and seemed to be enjoying watching everybody dance.

"Come on, you two get up and dance." Said Ray, Norah's husband.

They seemed to be a friendly couple.

"I'm enjoying myself just sitting and observing." Answered Gary.

"You don't plan on doing this all evening do you? They're playing a nice slow sexy dance. May I have this dance? Your old man won't mind will he?"

I could feel the tension mounting in Gary. So I got up and pulled on Gary's hand and said:

"I'm sorry, but this dance is for my handsome sexy husband." I told Ray.

"This is great." Gary replied. "You know I can't dance. I've never danced in my life. We are going to make fools of ourselves."

"Don't worry, Gary. It's easy. Just follow the beat of the music with a slow walk. We don't have to do anything fancy."

It was our first dance and I could feel everybody's eyes on us. Gary was a little nervous so I held him closer and moved him rhythmically and he just seemed to relax. I could feel his heart beating rapidly.

"I could get used to this. You feel so good in my arms." He whispered in my ear.

"You know something, Gary, for a guy who claims he never danced before you certainly have a lot of rhythm." I commented.

"You are pretty good yourself for an amateur."

We were lost in the magic of the beautiful music when someone yelled out:

"Hey, leave room, for the Holy Ghost."

Gary blushed and smiled as he pushed me away. I pulled him closer and said to the 'intruder',

"Are you jealous?"

"Why did you say that? Do you know him?" Gary said.

"No, of course not. I just wanted to show him that we can take a joke."

"I don't think I like that guy, he seems to be a wise guy." Gary replied.

I told him he was just trying to make light conversation to make us feel at home.

"They really are nice people and they are all trying to welcome us into their group. I really think they like us."

Then the song ended and we walked back to the table.

Gary said,

"I noticed that everybody dances with everybody else. Something strange seems to be going on. I don't like it."

I couldn't answer him because we had reached the table and I didn't want anyone to hear what I would say. He seemed to calm down and we actually stayed the whole evening. Gary liked the buffet. He enjoyed the exchange of gifts, and the visit from Santa Claus. Gary and I danced all of the slow dances. A few times someone asked me to dance, but I politely said that I only liked to dance with my husband. Mary could see that Gary was getting nervous and to change the tone she said:

"You two have to be the most handsome couple on the dance floor."

The crowd cheered and someone yelled out;

"Any time you get tired....."

Mary quickly interrupted and yelled out,

"Enough is enough. You're giving all the attention to Gary and Mel. What about the rest of us? I'm jealous."

I could not believe that Gary had not asked me once to go home early. It was one o'clock when we finally left. He must have really enjoyed himself. As we were leaving one of the couples asked us over for coffee. Gary thanked them and told them we had to go home.

Mary's husband told us that it was nice to have met us and he hoped we would come again.

"Wait Gary." He said." Do you want to go to the New Year's Eve dance? If you do, get your tickets as soon as possible. I only have a few left."

I was astonished. Gary bought the tickets. What was happening to my Gary? Was he seeing a doctor without my knowledge? I didn't dare mention it to him. I was afraid to break the magic spell.

When we got home we were pleased to hear that things had worked out well with the baby-sitter. Gary took her home and I got ready for bed. When Gary came home I could hear him puttering in the kitchen. I was pleasantly surprised when he brought me a cup of tea. I thanked him and told him I had had a wonderful time.

"It was much better than I had expected. The only thing I didn't like is how everyone was staring at you. The men seemed to want to get their paws all over you." Gary said.

"Of course not, Gary," I replied. "They were just trying to be friendly. You should be proud. I don't know if you think that you are lucky but I don't belong to anyone else but you. Let others look and you say to yourself,

"They're jealous and I'm proud."

I knew this wasn't accurate, but I had to say something to offset his jealousy.

I was sure no one was envious. Most of them enjoyed a much better life than ours.

"You know Gary, it was terrible of you to say that the couples who were mingling and dancing with others must have been unfaithful. That was a terrible accusation. You can be in love with your partner and have a good time dancing with someone else. That's where trust comes in. If you dance with someone else, I know you are mine and you are coming back to me because I trust you."

Gary fired back and said:

"Look kid, what makes you an authority on trust and love? You have your opinions and I have mine. Say whatever you want but I wouldn't trust you alone with any of those guys and I still love you. You are wrong! I can love with all of my heart and not trust. Goodnight! It's late."

21

I t was one week before Christmas and Gary had not mentioned anything about the membership. The children wouldn't be able to go to the Christmas party. Part of me wanted to mention it to Gary and part of me was fearful. After all he had given in and taken me to the dance and hadn't been moody nor lost his temper for the past couple of weeks. I wasn't going to push for more. I had never mentioned the party to the children so they couldn't be upset over what they didn't expect. I'd bring up the subject after the holidays. I really wanted the membership for the summertime.

It was such a busy week. I had to do the last minute shopping, wrapping, baking, and cooking. We had invited Gary's parents for Christmas dinner. I was very happy about that but they must have been shocked. It was the first invitation to dinner that they had ever received from us.

Christmas Eve was more family time for us. We spent a quiet night by the fire. We read the children some stories and we snacked on Christmas goodies. We put them to bed early in anticipation of Santa's visit. Gary and I placed all of the toys and presents under the tree. We were happy to sit and admire our work. Gary remarked,

"Wow! I think we overdid it."

I was in the kitchen getting the stuffing ready for the turkey when the telephone rang. It was Mary. She wanted us to go over to her house for a holiday drink. I asked Gary and he replied,

"Definitely not! What are you planning to do with the kids? Are you going to leave them alone?"

"How about if I invite them over here? I asked.

"Absolutely not! You know we have to go to bed early. We have a big day tomorrow and the kids will be up at the crack of dawn."

I made my excuses with Mary and wished her a Merry Christmas. I finished my work in the kitchen and went to join Gary in the family room by the fire. He said,

"Let's each open a present without the presence of the children?"

"That's a great idea!" I replied.

He picked out a gift and I went to get one for him. I was excited. He had really bought me a present on his own. He gave me a great big box. He told me that I had to guess. I couldn't for the life of me begin to imagine what it was. I told him that I couldn't guess. Finally I opened the box. There was series of boxes that I continued to open until I got to a small box which contained a beautiful expensive watch.

"Read the guarantee that goes with it." Gary insisted.

I unfolded the paper and saw that it was a membership to the club. In my enthusiasm I almost knocked Gary over as I thanked him and hugged him.

"Hey, let me open your present."

"It can't be compared to yours."

"Now, I know Mel, that you have no money."

He didn't know I had managed to save money from the weekly shopping allowance. He opened up his gift. It was a clock radio and he seemed to be quite happy. He must have been thinking of the radio he had smashed in one of his rages.

Gary and I did not belong to an established religion. We believed in God but we never participated in any formal services. Sometimes I wished that we had belonged to a church. Maybe prayer would have helped me cope with all the things that I had to endure. I could hear many cars going to midnight mass and I wished that I were going. I had many things to be grateful for lately.

"God, please hear my prayers. Help Gary. Help us all as a family. I will try to be a better wife."

What a madhouse it was on Christmas morning. The children and Bosco were going wild opening packages, playing with toys, and just plain having fun. I could see that Gary was getting pale and perspiring profusely. I was going to suggest that he go to the store for me. He got up and went into the kitchen clutching his head. I ran toward him. I forgot that he did not like to be disturbed when he had these strange headaches. I reached him and I asked him if I could help him. This only enraged him and he yelled at me as he shoved me aside.

He ran out of the house and drove off in his truck. I went into the bathroom so the children wouldn't see me crying. Thankfully, they were so busy enjoying their new toys they didn't notice we were not in the room. I was worried about Gary's parents. What would they think when they came to dinner if Gary wasn't there? I washed my face, put on a smile and walked into the family room. I wasn't going to spoil this almost perfect day.

The children and I readied the room and the table for the dinner. I asked them to be quiet because their father had a headache. I had everything under control, the room was beautifully decorated and the turkey and the vegetables were cooked to perfection. I decided to go to my room to get dressed. I was really worried and afraid. As I was imagining the worst, my husband appeared in the doorway. I ran into his arms, started to cry, and told him I was so happy he was there.

He hugged me but he didn't say anything. Finally he said we had to hurry to get ready before his parents came. The visit and the dinner went on without a glitch. We had an almost perfect Christmas holiday.

22

After Christmas, we started preparing for the New Year. Gary seemed to be going back to his old ways. He was probably getting more frequent headaches and he seemed to have a need to start an argument with me. He wouldn't help with any chores. He was sarcastic and accusatory. I knew enough to ignore him. It was really a dilemma for me. Answering him would get him angry and ignoring him would make him sexually demanding. I knew he would not stop his behavior until he had attacked me in some way.

One night he got what he subconsciously wanted. I don't know what the exact reason for his explosion was. It was late one evening and the children had gone to bed. He said something to me that I didn't understand because I was reading a book. All of a sudden, he slapped the book out of my hand and stood over me ranting and raging as he yelled,

"How dare you treat me as though I were part of the furniture? You care more about your fantasy sex novels than about my needs."

What started out as a rape sex event turned into a consensual one. I was so weak and he knew how to take advantage of me. There were not too many occasions, if any, when I had been able to resist him. He subjected me to all kinds of perverted acts and humiliations. I am embarrassed to admit that I loved every minute of it. He kept coming after me until I thought that I would pass out. I begged him to stop but he continued until he was exhausted and fell asleep. I couldn't even be angry with him. We seemed, in my mind, to deserve each other.

On New Year's Eve we had a great time at the party. Gary had a few drinks and was in a mellow mood. He rarely drank and when he did it was very little; however, that night the drinks were on the house. Thank God Gary wasn't mean when he drank. On the contrary, he was more sociable and he even had a sense of humor. He got up and danced a jitterbug with me. 'Miracle of miracles! I thought of buying some alcoholic drinks for the house. We both enjoyed the evening and each other.

It was midnight and the crowd was celebrating. They were all singing and yelling "Happy New Year". I had never experienced the likes of this. It was delightful. Then I noticed everybody kissing everyone. Gary looked at me and kissed me. That kiss seemed to embody everything that was good about Gary. We were oblivious to the rest of the crowd. We were brought back to reality when blaring horns and cries from the rest of the group interrupted our 'almost' passionate moment. I wrapped my arms around Gary until he regained his composure. We made light of the situation. I told them that our New Year's resolution was 'never to be separated'. Gary made a joke that wasn't particularly funny when he said:

"We've got something hard between us that we must resolve."

The crowd exploded with laughter. I had to join in because Gary looked adorable with his ruffled hair and his ridiculous hat. I hoped he wouldn't remember half of what had happened.

The women were all lined up to kiss Gary and wish him a Happy New Year, and I was feeling a little jealous. They said to me:

"No wonder you never want to go anywhere. I don't blame you. If I had a good-looking husband like yours, I wouldn't want to share him either. I'd keep him under lock and key."

Mary, sensing my uneasiness told me not to bother with their comments. It was the liquor talking. I accepted her explanation and made sure the men who wished me a Happy New Year kissed me on the cheek. I did not want Gary to overhear any comments about my kissing ability.

After the dance, much to my surprise, Gary agreed to go to an after dance party at Lois's house. I was really exhausted and I wanted to go home but I didn't dare say anything. There was no reason to get home early because we had made arrangements for the babysitter to sleep overnight. So, we went to the party. Gary and Ray were the life of the party. I had never seen him in this mood before. It was sad that he couldn't be pleasant when he was sober. They would find out soon enough about his 'true' character. Maybe I was a little jealous. Finally, I said,

"Gary, let's go home. I'm tired."

"What! It's too early and I'm having fun. Come and play this game with us."

"Come on." Everyone chimed in. "We're playing charades."

"No, thanks." I answered. "I'm too tired. I'm not used to staying up this late."

"Okay, Mel, you go home. I'll meet you later." Gary yelled out.

I was hurt and angry. I couldn't believe that Gary was sending me home alone at this hour. Mary came to the rescue and told me she and her husband were about to leave and they would take me home. I decided to leave and I hoped that he wouldn't lose control of his temper and make a fool of himself after I left.

When Gary came home I was sound asleep. The kids

woke me up in the morning, and asked me how come their father was sleeping on the couch and how come he was still all dressed. I told them he had fallen asleep watching television. I went downstairs, woke him up, and brought him upstairs. He still looked drunk. I gave him two aspirins.

The baby-sitter had breakfast with the children and me and then walked home. Gary didn't get up until late afternoon. He didn't remember my coming home alone and his going to a party. He was under the impression we had come home together. I didn't tell him anything different. He told me he didn't know what was in the drinks they had served because he felt 'horny' and that was all he could think about.

"What did you do woman? Did you tease the hell out of me and then not finish what you had started?"

"I just remember one incident." I replied, "You were more than ready on the dance floor when I kissed you."

"Check me out. I'm more than ready now." He said.

"You pick the worst times. The children are all alone downstairs." I said.

"It's more fun this way. I'll check the kids in the playroom."

"Really? You're in no position to go out of this room Just look at yourself. I can see the children pointing and asking you what's that." I said. He replied:

"Alright, Miss No-It-All, you go check on them and come back. I want to make love to you right now."

I went downstairs and told the children that their father and I had some important things to discuss and they were not to disturb us unless it was an emergency. We would be in the bedroom. I told them I would give them ice cream when I came down. I then went upstairs like a dutiful wife. I wasn't fooling anyone. I almost ran upstairs with great anticipation. There

I found Gary in the nude. I was thinking of how perverted I was. I told him that I was an animal. He told me that he knew it and proceeded to strip me of my clothes. The rest was as fulfilling as usual. Another trophy added to my collection.

23

I t was springtime, my favorite season of the year. Gary hadn't had too many episodes. He was always more careful when I was pregnant. We went to two more dances. During the last dance, we sneaked out and we went to our favorite little parking spot to relive and revive old memories. Everyone was worried and began to look for us. They searched everywhere. They even went to our house to look for the car. We got back to the hall before they could call the police. Everyone teased us and Gary seemed to enjoy his newfound notoriety. Gary was in a good mood and agreed to go to Mary's house for coffee after the dance. I was furious. I was in no condition to go to a party. My clothes were all rumpled, my hair was a mess and I was tired. I combed my hair and straightened my clothes and pretended I was pleased. When I got to the house I claimed the bathroom first asserting that I was pregnant and should be given priority.

While I was in the bathroom I could hear Gary brag about our sex lives. He was volunteering information about the greatness of making love to a pregnant wife in the cramped quarters of a car. Gary said,

"There we were all alone in the woods. We could hear the crickets, the frogs, and an owl hooting.....and..."

I was so embarrassed. I didn't want to come out of the bathroom. Everybody was laughing and telling Gary what a lucky guy he was. One of the men told him he could never get his wife to go parking because she was an old 'stick in the mud'.

Mary called everybody to the kitchen for snacks. I took advantage of this moment and came out without being too noticed. I just gave Gary a dirty look. Everyone was kind enough to drop the subject.

When we got home, Gary questioned me about the dirty look. I replied angrily,

"You know damn well what it was for. How dare you embarrass me so? I can't figure you out. Either you ignore people and don't talk, or you talk too much. There's no happy medium for you. I never thought you would ever share intimate details of our sex lives with anyone. I don't know how I'm going to face Mary this week."

I had crossed the line. Gary came towards me in a rage. I continued,

"See what I mean. Here's another side of you. Now you're going into a rage and you are going to beat me up. Go ahead and smack me, you coward. The baby and I are defenseless. I'd like to see you attack someone your own size. In fact I almost did once. Remember Bob? He almost beat you when I was single. He spared you because he knew I would be upset. That was a sorry mistake!.."

"Shut up! Shut up! You bitch." He screamed as he grabbed my shoulders.

He was shaking me so hard I thought my head was going to come off. I don't know what possessed me but I continued yelling at him and telling him what a sad example of a man he was. He slapped me in the mouth and threw me on the bed. I still kept on telling him off. It was as though I had opened the dam and all of the things welled up inside me just came gushing out. I couldn't stop and he continued abusing me. I didn't feel a thing.

Gary had never witnessed this side of me and it scared him. All of a sudden he changed and begged me to be quiet.

"Please Mel, don't say anymore. You're driving me crazy and you're hurting me with your words. Please stop it. If you don't, I know I will hurt you. I can feel it coming on. Please, please stop."

I started to tell him that I was sorry, but as soon as I did, he put his big hand over my mouth. The impact was so hard I thought I would swallow my teeth. He dragged me to the bureau, took out a handkerchief, shoved it in my mouth, and tied it with a kerchief. I thought I would vomit. I could hardly breathe. He then said,

"You are going to listen to me after you calm down and after I get rid of my headache."

I don't know which horror movie had inspired Gary. He tied me up with a rope and put me in the closet. He blocked the door with a chair. I wasn't afraid of the closet, but I was frightened by the fact that I couldn't breathe. I managed to relax and to push the handkerchief to the front of my mouth and that enabled me to catch my breath. I had plenty of time to think.

Here I was seven months pregnant tied up in a closet. In my sick mind I blamed myself for the predicament I was in. I knew Gary suffered from these severe headaches brought on by confrontation. I shouldn't have been so upset by Gary's behavior at the party. I should not have told him all of those awful things even if they were true. I should have said nothing. I should have realized that he was really trying to change his behavior and I had not helped. I was so confused. I didn't know anymore. Was I right? Was I wrong? I finally fell asleep and awoke when Gary came to the door.

"Are you ready to shut up and listen to me?"

I nodded yes. He untied me and gave me a glass of water.

"Mel, you said some terrible things to me. I never thought you hated me so much."

"Gary, I don't hate you." I said.

Before I could say more, he pointed to the handkerchief and I got the message.

"I don't want to repeat this scene ever again, because the next time you won't be so lucky. I almost went out of my mind and I don't know what prevented me from hurting you more."

He said this with so much emphasis. He wanted to make sure I got the message. I had to listen to him or I would be in serious jeopardy. He continued,

"I've been trying really hard to change. You have to admit I have shown some improvement. In the future, if you don't want me to go into any more rages don't provoke them. I'm going to have to punish you. I want to make sure you learned your lesson."

I could just imagine what the punishment would be. It had to be something sexual. I was very familiar with his demands. He would command me to do all sorts of perverted things and be his slave. He would torture me, hurt me, and watch me beg. He would get joy out of arousing my passion, stand up abruptly, pleasure himself, and leave the room laughing hysterically. He was one sick person and I was no better for accepting his behavior. I didn't worry too much about what he was going to do to 'punish' me because I was sure he had done it to me before.

The club had one more dance for the year and Gary refused to go. He was inflexible and he would not change his mind. I was really upset, but as usual I said nothing. I told Mary I didn't think that I should go because I tired very easily.

On Saturday, Gary hadn't changed his mind. He was working outside in the yard and I overheard him talking to Paul who was asking him if he were going to the dance. Gary told him that his 'old' lady wasn't feeling well but he'd miss the fun at the dance. What a liar he was! I still did not know what the real reason for his refusal was, but I soon found out.

"I have the whole evening planned." Gary said. "Tonight you're going to do everything I command you to do."

"What do you mean tonight? ' I answered. "Don't I always do as you say?"

"There you go again." He said as he raised his hand to slap me. "Don't smart mouth me. Haven't you learned your lesson yet? Now I want you to tell me you're sorry."

I obediently apologized.

"That's better." He said. "We didn't go to the dance because on this night I will punish you. You have it coming to you. Tonight you will do as I tell you."

He had me be his slave all night. First he had me pop corn. He then turned into a charmer when he asked me to massage his back as he watched television. During this massage he started taking his clothes off. He paraded around me in the nude as he invented little things for me to do. He finally handed me a jar of cream. I had been on that route before. I had to put it on every part of his body as I massaged him. He returned the favor by doing the same thing to me after he tenderly undressed me. After an hour of caressing he decided he wanted me to bathe him in the tub. I told him I had a hard time bathing the children because my belly got in the way.

"You can get in the tub with me." He replied.

"Ridiculous! How are we both going to fit in the tub?" I could get an infection. The doctor told me to shower and not to bathe in a tub."

I must have said too much because I could see he was getting upset and I knew what that meant. He grabbed me and yelled,

"Okay, you bitch with the big mouth. I offered you an easy job, but you had to have your own way. I was going to gently get the cream off and then bathe you. You don't appreciate anything I try to do for you, no matter how I try. You are nothing but ungrateful. I thought that at this stage of your pregnancy you'd want a milder version of lovemaking, but you're so oversexed. I'll be glad to oblige. You asked for it and you're going to get it."

He was so passionate. He was like a crazed maniac. He put me into all kinds of contorted positions and continued on and on until I was ready to pass out. I can honestly say it was the first time I did not enjoy his attempts to arouse me. I screamed and cried and the bastard thought that it was from joy. He continued to pounce on me until I finally grabbed the back of his hair and pulled with much force. He kept telling me to control myself. He thought I was acting out of passion and so he responded with more intense and rigorous behavior.

"What's the matter with you Mel? I've never seen you this wild before. What's wrong? What do you want me to do?"

"Leave me alone." I answered him as I sobbed.

When would I learn to keep my thoughts to myself? He jumped on top of me and satisfied himself. It was over. Thank God. I hurt so much and I couldn't move. He had the nerve to ask me,

"Was it good?"

"Good?" I answered.

I had enough sense to stop myself and not tell him how I really felt. I made my way to the shower and just let the water massage my aching body. As I was lathering myself I had a sudden searing pain. I screamed and Gary came in. He carried me to the couch and the pain subsided. I asked him to please dress me because I knew I would have the baby that night. I was right, in the middle of the night the contractions started again.

I called Laurie and asked her to please come over and stay with the children until Gary got back from the hospital. I told her she wouldn't have to stay too long because Gary never stayed.

"Don't worry about it. Tomorrow is Sunday and Jack is home. So, tell Gary not to rush." She told me.

When I got to the hospital, I had a hard time explaining my bruised body and the raw condition of other body parts. It was quite embarrassing to listen to what the doctor had to tell me. Luckily, I didn't have a difficult delivery.

My fifth child was a girl whom I named Melissa. No more children's names that began with the letter 'K'. Missy came into this world under strange circumstances that I never forgot.

ummertime was upon us and I was back into a regular routine. I was feeling fine. I had worked out a schedule with Mary so that we could spend more time at the beach and playground. We did all of our work in the morning and then spent the rest of the day swimming, lounging, and playing with the children. I'd get home early enough to prepare a hearty meal for Gary and the family.

Gary seemed to be spending less time at the shop. He had taken off a few Saturdays and a few weeknights. He had hired somebody to run the shop for him. I didn't know why. He never told me anything about his business or his finances. I had no idea how much income we had.

I had two great friends, Laurie and Mary. Because of them I had the greatest summer ever. Little did I know that it was the best I would ever have. We participated in so many fun activities. The club sponsored them and we attended most of them. The clambake was one of the most memorable ones. We all enjoyed it. Gary even worked with the neighbors preparing and serving the food. The children were invited so the women remained sober and kept them from the kegs of beer. It was a different story for the men. It was apparent my husband was having his share of the beer.

After supper, some of the women were going home to put their children to bed and leave them with a baby-sitter. There was a whole evening of partying planned for the adults. Some of the husbands went with their wives but not Gary. I decided to go home alone to bring the children. It was just as well because if Gary came home with me he would have something else on his mind and we would never come back. I didn't want to miss the party.

We had a great time. We danced, sang, and played games. I decided to drink draft beer and I was slightly intoxicated. No one was sober. At one o'clock in the morning Ray had a bright idea. He yelled out:

"It's so damned hot. Who's brave enough to go skinny dipping?"

"What's that?" I said.

"Come with us, we'll show you."

I looked to make sure Gary was coming along. He certainly was and he wasn't walking too steadily. No one was. By the time we got to the beach I was pretty sure I knew what skinny dipping meant. Some of the men had already stripped off their clothes and run into the ocean. At first the women went in with their clothes on.

The men were egging us on and telling us to take our clothes off. They were coming after us and some were not grabbing their own wives.

"Whoops, sorry." Said Ray as he grabbed me.

It really wasn't a wild party. Nobody touched anybody indecently. They were just having fun throwing the women up in the air. Then Bob said,

"Come on girls, it's not fair. Here we are buck naked and you still have your clothes on. What do you say? Be good sports."

I looked at Gary and he said that it was okay. It felt great.

"Well do we or don't we girls?" I said.

"Why not? Bev said.

She began flinging her clothes in the air. I was drunk but not enough to know that I had to make sure I knew where my clothes were when I got out of the water. I said to Mary,

"Let's take our clothes off and put them on the dock so we can put them on before we come out of the water."

She agreed and all the other women followed suit. Gary was right it did feel great. We knew that the boys were up to no good. They were huddled in a group laughing and gesturing. We were aware of their actions. We felt so liberated we didn't mind. We weren't too concerned. All of a sudden they had disappeared. They were swimming towards us. They held each one of us in the air and let us down. They did this several times. Whoever picked me up grabbed me in an inappropriate manner a few times. One of the woman yelled out that she had grabbed somebody's 'pistol' under water. Things were beginning to get out of control.

"These pigs are playing nasty games with us and getting turned on. We had better put a stop to it." Mary said.

We swam to our husbands and finally the playing quieted down. Some of us remained in the water and others went on the beach. It ended up being a great night and no harm had been done. I was happy because I wouldn't have wanted anything to ruin the evening. Summer was over and it had been fantastic!

26

It was the beginning of fall and school time for the children. I had two of them in school. Kevin was in the first grade and Karen was in the kindergarten. I really missed them. They were a big help with the other children. They grew up too fast. Before I knew it, they would all be in school.

We went through the usual spell of diseases, but that winter we had a terrible bout with the chicken pox. Even little Missy was covered with scabs. I was so tired. Looking after them and trying to keep up with the housework was almost impossible. Gary didn't offer any comfort, help, or sympathy. In fact, he would leave earlier than normal in the morning and come home later. He couldn't stand to see his kids covered with scabs.

One of the reasons I was so far behind in all of my work was because I had to make sure that nothing interfered with services rendered to the 'king' of the house. His meals had to be well prepared; his clothes had to be ironed just so; and his laundry had to be washed and folded perfectly. He purposely messed up the drawers of his bureau so that I would have to fix them daily. He just loved aggravating me. I was feeling sorry for myself. I hadn't gone outside in weeks and I hadn't seen Mary or Laurie in what seemed to be forever.

Oh, sweet revenge, Gary came down with the chicken pox three weeks before Christmas. I had never heard of an adult contracting the disease but the doctor confirmed it. Gary had chicken pox. He had to be quite sick to allow the doctor to come to the house and examine him. He looked horrible. His face and body were covered with scabs. He couldn't shave. I had to bathe him with special soap. He was so demanding and most obnoxious. He was worse than the children. He wouldn't come out of his room and he constantly called me to wait on him for some reason or other. It was almost more than I could bear. What a difference this holiday would be from the previous Christmas.

We had succeeded in getting some shopping done before Gary got sick. He was now on his way to a good recovery, but he chose to play the part of a helpless invalid to gain my attention. It didn't work. That evening, I told him I was going shopping within the hour.

"No way, you are not going to leave me here alone in this condition." He lamented.

"You have no choice. You have to let me go. You're not well enough to go out. The doctor said that it would be two weeks before you could go back to work."

"Your duty is here with me." He said.

"My duty is also to the kids. Just because you're sick, doesn't mean that we have to punish the children and not have gifts for them for Christmas. I only have two weeks left to do the shopping." I replied.

"As far as I'm concerned," he said sarcastically, "I don't feel like celebrating Christmas and don't start with your smart mouth."

I started crying. I didn't have any Christmas spirit either but I kept thinking of the children. How would they react if we did nothing for Christmas? They had had such a great time last year. I felt so helpless and I knew if I defied Gary I would pay for it dearly. My children meant so much to me. I had to find a way for them to have a good holiday.

"Okay Gary, I'm not going to start with my smart mouth. Please, honey, listen to me. That's all I want you to do. You say that you love me more than anything else in this world. Then, how can you stand to see me like this? Can't you see how much weight I have lost? How tired I am? I don't get any sympathy or help from you."

"I put in my time and share of work at the mill and at the shop and you don't hear me complaining. The trouble with you is that you're a spoiled brat. Just because I helped you a couple of times, you expect me to do it all the time." He replied.

"Gary, that's not the point. I don't mind doing my share of the work. This is different. The kids and you have been sick and I am running ragged trying to keep up with all the work. You say you love me and yet you want me to wait on you hand and foot when you're beginning to feel better. It's very evident that I am not feeling well but you are still demanding. That's not what I want to discuss with you. I want to talk about Christmas. I know that you don't have any holiday spirit and I don't blame you, but for the children's sake we have to make an effort."

Gary interrupted and said,

"The kids have to learn to take the good with the bad."

"Gary, they're so young. What's wrong with shielding them from evil things as long as we can? God knows that they will face enough problems in their lives. We've had more than our share."

"What the hell do you mean by that remark? After all I have done for you. See what I mean? I have given you everything, a beautiful home, money, food, and a new car. What more do you want? There is no satisfying you, woman. I'm going to have to be stricter." He screamed.

I wanted to scream a never-ending cry of despair. I just couldn't talk to this guy. All I wanted to do was solve our holiday problem. We were driving in different vehicles, and were going nowhere fast. I couldn't take any more so I ran out of the room.

"Get back here." He yelled.

"Go to hell, "Gary" I replied as I grabbed my coat and car keys. I drove to Laurie's house.

"I know that I'm a little early for shopping, but I just had to get out of the house. This has been the worst winter of my life. I've been shut in so much because of the kids and now Gary."

"You poor kid. "She said.

That was all I needed. One kind word had opened up the dam of tears. I burst out crying and ran out of the house. I got into the car and drove endlessly and aimlessly. Finally I came to my senses and the thought of the children confronted me. I knew Gary wouldn't abuse them. I felt like a zombie. I was driving and I didn't know where I was. I decided to ask for directions at the gas station. I hadn't driven too far. I was only an hour away from home.

The realization of what had just happened frightened me. I was afraid of going back home. Gary would kill me. Then again I knew that Gary loved his children and he would not leave them motherless. I took a deep breath and headed home.

On my way back, I stopped and did all of the shopping. I was ready for all his tirades, but I had finished my shopping. I was proud of myself. I had succeeded in buying all of the gifts for the children and my in-laws. In spite of what was waiting for me at home, I was satisfied. When I left the store, I even had the nerve to buy a Christmas tree.

I sat frozen to my seat in the driveway for a long time. I was terrified. Gary must have heard me pull up. In fact I knew he was watching. Finally I jumped out of the car. Gary was at the door and he looked concerned. He asked me what I was doing.

"Gary, I almost didn't come back to you. I was going to leave you with the kids and never come back."

"You wouldn't dare." He said.

"Don't give me that chance again." I said. "I will come back to you right now, if you promise not to hurt me."

I burst into tears. I was so angry with myself for being so weak, but I couldn't help it. He put his arms around me and led me to the door and said,

"Welcome home, Melanie. I promise you that things will be better."

Once I was inside the house I had a complete meltdown. I cried and cried and lay down on the couch. Gary told me to rest and that he would make me a cup of tea. Then Gary took all the gifts and the tree out of the car. He never complained. He remarked that I had chosen a nice tree. We would decorate it the following night.

I was so wrapped up in my own emotions and feelings that I had forgotten about Gary's illness. He certainly did not look too healthy. He had worried about me all night and had just done a great deal of physical work. I asked him how he was feeling and he answered,

"Not bad, now that I have you home."

"Gary, I'm sorry, but I guess I couldn't take any more. I just had to get away for a while. I really feel as though I'm on the verge of a nervous breakdown." I said.

"Please don't say that Mel. I couldn't stand it if anything ever happened to you. I'll try to give you a hand as much as I can, until you feel better. I know it's been rough on you and that I've been too selfish to help. Let's try to forget tonight and these past three weeks and concentrate more on the coming holiday. What do you say?"

"Sounds great to me." I replied.

Gary tried very hard to please me. He was able to shave again and it made him look almost healthy. It was good to have my handsome husband back.

We managed to have a good Christmas. It didn't compare to the previous year, but it was acceptable. The fact that I was not feeling well and Gary had been sick contributed to the lackluster. Gary's parents came to the dinner and Irene was concerned about my looks. I was so thin, but I assured her I was not pregnant. She looked relieved.

27

It was one week before the New Year's Eve party and Gary hadn't decided if we were going or not. I knew Carl had saved two tickets for us. Mary and he were still hoping we would go with them. I was happy they thought enough of us to want us to go with them. Two days before the dance Carl called Gary on the phone and said:

"I've got two tickets to the dance. We'd love to have you come. What do you say? We had such a great time last year. It would be good for you to get out of the house. You've had your share of sickness this year."

"I'll have to check with Melanie. It's up to her. I don't want to push her. She hasn't been feeling well and she won't go to the doctor. Thanks for thinking of us. I'll let you know later this evening."

I definitely wanted to go. It had been so long since we had had a good time together. Our sex life was practically nonexistent. Gary didn't like it but he learned to live with it. A couple of times he started to lose it. He began accusing me of having an affair and that was why I didn't want 'him'. I didn't even acknowledge the accusations. I was not the 'wild' woman he was accustomed to. I tried to tell him that it was temporary. I let him rant on, but I was slightly concerned myself. I had always been able to respond to Gary's demands even when he beat me. Maybe the problem was that he was acting like a normal person instead of a brute. I was not accustomed to being treated nicely. Then I told myself I wasn't thinking clearly. The problem had to be that I wasn't feeling well. I was just too tired and exhausted to make love and that was it.

Gary told me about his conversation with Carl. He asked me if I really wanted to go. I did not have to say 'yes' just to please him. I answered him and said,

"I really would like to go, if you don't mind. I think that we owe it to ourselves to have a little fun."

Gary returned Carl's call and told him we would be attending the dance.

The night of the dance Gary reminded me that it was time to get ready. He asked me if I needed help putting the children to bed.

"If not, I'll get my shower out of the way and then you can have the bathroom all to yourself."

"Okay, Gary, 'I've almost finished with the kids. I'll keep them up until you finish showering. Then you can spend a little time with them before their bedtime."

When Gary came down in his bathrobe, I felt a flutter and actually blushed when Gary's eyes met mine. It was great to have that 'old' feeling again. I thought this would never happen again. I was all tingly inside and I kind of wished I had already put the children to bed. I was sure Gary had picked up on my vibes.

I decided to take a bubble bath instead of a shower. I lay there daydreaming about my husband. I decided to rinse off when Gary came in.

"Hi, are you enjoying yourself? I hate to spoil your fun but it's getting late. If you still want to go..."

He said this as he was disrobing. My pulse started to race and I couldn't think straight. I wanted him so. Gary extended his arms and gently pulled me out of the tub. He kissed me ever so gently. It had been a long time since we had experienced these feelings. He carried me into the bedroom and we shared a night of unbelievable passion. We went on for hours, and I didn't give the dance a second thought until Gary said,

"Would you like to dance Mrs.D.?"

"Oh, my God, the dance, the baby-sitter. What are we going to do?"

"Don't worry. I took care of everything. I called Carl and the baby-sitter and made my apologies. I put the children to bed when I saw the look in your eyes. Mel, it's been so long. I just couldn't pass up this opportunity.

"Are you sorry?" He asked as he kissed my neck.

"I couldn't be happier."

I was determined to show him how pleased I was, and I did. I thought he would go out of his mind with excitement. Finally he said to me,

"If I were to die tonight, I wouldn't have any regrets. You have made me happy beyond words. Melanie, I love you with all my heart."

28

After the holidays, the children seemed to fall into a good healthy routine. Gary and I had a closer relationship. I was regaining some of my strength and slowly becoming my old self. As a result, everyone was more relaxed. It had been a long trying winter. They had to contend with the rages and mood swings of their father, and my poor health. I promised myself I'd make it up to them. It wouldn't be too difficult now that it was spring and I was feeling much better.

Gary took me to the movies and to a couple of dances. Things were looking up and I was feeling on top of the world. We often went parking and Gary held on to me so tightly. It was as though he was afraid he would lose me. Sometimes, I would have to remind him he was hurting me. He would apologize. He seemed to be lost in thought. Then he would tell me he'd like to stop time and continue life just the way it was at that particular moment. He didn't want to get any older, he liked the children just the way they were. He continued,

"I love our life just the way it is. I wouldn't change anything in our sex life. I don't have so many headaches. Everything seems so perfect. I just want to stop right now. How do you feel Mel?"

"We've come such a long way. I'm hoping that all the suffering we've endured was for a purpose-a better future. Gary, we don't have to be afraid. We have weathered the past we can face the future. I am not afraid of you any more because

I know you really love me. I know how hard you have been trying to change and that means the world to me. I know that you care deeply for your family. Do you understand what I'm trying to tell you?"

"Of course," he said, "I must not be afraid of the future. If we have come this far without killing each other we should be able to face what the future has in store for us."

"We can't ask for anything better. God willing, I'll always be by your side."

It was the first deep discussion we had ever had without ending in a serious fight. Gary never wanted to share his feelings with me but that night he did and I didn't know what was responsible for the change. It was as though he had a premonition of some impending life changing event. He was so melancholic, so I held him in my arms and we continued to talk until it developed into a lovemaking match that complimented our warm and tender mood.

Saint Patrick's day was just a couple of weeks away and Gary was busy with Carl planning the Irish dance at the club. He was now getting involved with activities and thoroughly enjoying himself. I couldn't wait for the dance. The women had decorated the hall, and the men were cooking corn beef and cabbage. There was even a keg of green draft beer. I had never heard of green beer. I hadn't heard much about anything in my cocoon. We lived in a shell and lately, Gary and I came out once in a while.

We had a great time at the dance. Gary drank enough to be mellow. The little bit I had made me horny. I put Gary through hell during the dances. He didn't seem to mind. We shared precious moments and feelings during our slow dances. Soon the slow dances were over and a polka brought us back to reality. Gary was being a good sport and he took a stab at trying to dance. What a disaster! We were turning and laughing until Laurie and Jack came to our rescue. We exchanged partners and they taught each of us the dance steps.

Sexy Gail came up to me and asked my permission to dance with my husband. It was a slow dance. She said,

"I've been watching Gary dance. I just l-o-v-e the way he moves. You don't mind do you?"

"Not if he doesn't." I lied.

I was hoping that Gary would refuse her but much to my chagrin he accepted. Gary was trying to keep her at arms' length but that's not what Gail wanted. I saw her wrap her arms around his neck and rub her big bosom against him. I was fuming. I wanted to go scratch her eyes out. I saw her rolling her hips trying to get my husband excited. I remember what happened when I acted this way. It had better not happen with her. I was so upset and angry.

Jack was watching and anticipated my next move so he came to the rescue and asked me to dance. He was trying to get me to calm down. The music was comforting and I managed to relax a little. What a smooth dancer Jack was. I could see Gail trying to seduce my husband. I remember her telling me once,

"Boy does Gary turn me on. You are some lucky lady. Anytime you want to switch partners, just let me know."

Ordinarily I would have been flattered. I was envied because of my sexy husband, but that night was different. She was not just talking. She was acting out her fantasies. After the dance, Jack thanked me and I told him that he was a great dancer. I started looking for my husband. It was dark and I couldn't see him. I found him in the corner with her still hanging on to him. I saw him trying to walk away and she was pulling his hand. She led him to an alcove and she was putting her arms around his neck. I heard her say,

"I missed not wishing you a Happy New Year at the dance. We had such a good time last year. Remember?"

She didn't even give him time to answer. She kissed him passionately groaning and saying,

"Oh Gary.."

I didn't give her a chance to continue. I grabbed her by the neck. She yelled and I pulled some of the hair from her hairpiece. She looked so ridiculous. I started to laugh and said,

"No more dreams of a passionate encounter with my husband."

I wasn't even angry. I said to Gary,

"You bastard, you had better not be aroused. I would never forgive you for that."

He was a little shocked. We both looked at each other and laughed. Of course if he had been turned on, it would have been a different scenario. Gail was humiliated. She looked like a damn fool with half of her hair on the floor. Gary and I were laughing and that did not add to her good state of mind. I looked at Gary and asked him if he had enjoyed his little escapade. He said,

"Not at all. In fact she kisses like a fish."

It was easier to believe him than it was to question him more. So I went into the warmth of his arms and gave him a tender kiss. We were drifting into our own little private world when someone yelled out,

"Hey, you two! The party is out here. We'll have an orgy later on."

"That sounds great." I answered,

I had no clue as to what 'orgy' meant. Gary looked at me and I knew that I had given the wrong answer. I told him that I really didn't know what an orgy was. Just then Kevin said,

"Right on, you're my kind of woman."

He got a hold of my hand and led me to the dance floor. Gary wasn't too pleased. He had never liked Kevin. I didn't want to be rude so I went along. Subconsciously I might have been giving Gary a taste of his own medicine.

We got home late but that didn't prevent us from making love for hours. Gary didn't hesitate to tell me how proud he was.

"Believe me Melanie, I didn't want her to kiss me. I was just about to push her when you pulled her away. You sure did pull her away! When you had her hair in your hand I could not help but laugh. Now I know that you really care for me. Come here and I'll show you how much I care for you."

During Holy Week, I got a surprise call from my brother. I hadn't seen him since my mother's funeral. I was happy to hear from him. He told me he was in town on business and he was staying the week. I invited him to come over for Easter dinner and to stay overnight. I was a little worried about Gary's reaction. My brother refused the offer to sleep over but he accepted the dinner invitation. He said his company was paying for the hotel accommodations. He told me,

"Thanks anyway, but the kids seem to like it here. They have a swimming pool, a game room and many activities to keep them busy. It's like a vacation for them. We'll be there for dinner if you don't mind. The children should really get to know each other. They are cousins."

"Great!" I said. "I'll expect you and your family on Sunday."

I gave him directions and hung up the phone. When I told Gary I could tell that he wasn't too pleased, but he did not say anything. He even helped me clean up the house.

Finally it was Sunday and everybody had arrived. It was a madhouse. He had four children and along with my five and the dog they were tearing up the place. I looked at Gary and noticed he was nervous.

"Dear God, please help him. Don't let him lose it and embarrass me. "I prayed.

Gary invited his brother-in-law into the family room to watch television. As he left he whispered to me,

"Try to keep those devils out of the room, please."

I was trying to prepare dinner and the children were running wild. Kevin kept asking me to let him go down to the beach with his cousins. He wanted to show them the playground and the ocean where he swam in the summer.

"Definitely not!" I said. "You know you are not allowed out of the yard. Let alone go down to the ocean."

"Please!" Begged his older cousin. "We'll watch him and we'll be right back."

"No, you don't understand. My children are not accustomed to leaving the yard and certainly not allowed to go to the beach by themselves. They certainly are not going to start now."

I continued getting things ready and trying to entertain a conversation with my sister-in-law. Kevin kept nagging me and begging to go. It was so unlike him. He could see I was very busy, and we had visitors, so he was a little more brazen. I almost slapped him. Finally I snapped and said,

"Kevin, get out of here before I lose my temper. Go ask your father. Maybe he will let you go."

That's exactly what Kevin did. He told his father I had told him to ask him for permission to go down to the beach. His father told him that was my domain. Kevin was back in the kitchen and said,

"Ma, Dad said it was up to you. Please, Ma, please! I don't see any harm in letting me go. Can I?"

"Shut up, Kevin or I'll slap you."

"I'll be right back, Dad said it was fine with him."

Finally, I gave in.

"You win, Kevin. I'll take care of you tonight. You had better make sure you don't go near the water. Come right back. Don't be long. Promise?"

All three of them agreed as they sauntered down the road.

When they got to the waterfront, Kevin spotted a boat at the end of the dock. He decided to investigate. His cousins warned him and told him not to go near it, but Kevin insisted on climbing onto the boat. When he jumped, the boat broke loose and moved away from the dock. The other two children panicked and told him to come back. He didn't have any oars and the boat was going upstream. Paul yelled to him to stay calm. He was going to get help from his father.

I was still busy in the kitchen when I heard all this commotion.

"Uncle Gary, come quick."

I saw my husband running down to the beach. I followed him and in my heart I knew something terrible had happened.

"Please, dear God, don't let anything happen to Kevin."

When I reached the beach I saw the most heart-wrenching scene I would ever witness in my lifetime. My husband was carrying our dead son out of the water. We tried everything to revive him to no avail. He was gone. Our seven-year old son was dead. We had never felt a greater sorrow. It was too much to bear. The rescue squad came and they were devastated also. I couldn't stop crying and I could not be consoled. I looked for my husband and saw him walking up the road toward the house. He was slumped over crying. I knew how he felt and I could not take away the pain. The children all gathered around me and cried. Some of them were too young to realize what had happened. Karen had the baby in her arms. I cradled both of them.

"I know, sweetheart. Don't be afraid to cry. Let it all out."

We walked back to the house and I didn't know what I would do. I lost all control when the rescue squad drove off with Kevin's body. I almost dropped Missy from my arms. Karen rescued her. I was crazed with sorrow and I kept screaming and yelling for Kevin.

"Please don't let it be true. Bring him back to me. What if he wakes up? He'll want to see his mommy."

I wanted to go to the hospital. He might call for me when he woke up. I refused to believe that he was dead. I was in complete denial.

"Please, let me go to my son. He's all alone."

Then I started to cry uncontrollably. I knew that Kevin was never going to wake up again. That thought hurt me so deeply. My chest ached my throat was throbbing and I couldn't stop myself. All I wanted was to be with my Kevin.

As I was trying to get to my car, someone was holding me back, but I kept screaming that I had to go. I had to be with my son. I was carried into the house. One of the neighbors took over the household duties.

Gary took off in his truck and made his way to the hospital. He made all the funeral arrangements. The funeral was incredibly sad. Gary was a broken man and I was no help at all. We would not and could not accept the fact that we would never see Kevin anymore.

After the funeral we never mentioned Kevin's name again. It was a forbidden topic. One day he slapped Karen because she started to talk about Kevin. I tried to console her as Gary drove away in his truck. He was unable to cope with his grief. I was not much better, but at least I tried to act normally for the sake of the other children. Gary just drifted further and further away into a world that didn't allow room for anyone.

He ignored me and he would have nothing to do with the children. His dog followed him everywhere and seemed to understand his sorrow.

30

Six months went by and nothing had changed. Gary had become a robot. He didn't allow anything or anyone into his little world of self-pity. He didn't have anything to do with his children or me. I didn't know what to do. I thought that I would go mad. I felt so sad and rejected. Many nights I cried myself to sleep when Gary was out.

One night, when I thought that Gary was at the shop, I put the children to bed and just sat on my bed. I began to think about Kevin and tried to relive all the memories from his birth to his death. I saw him in his crib as a baby. He was so adorable. I pictured him bringing me his projects. He was so proud of his work. I saw him with his father who was beaming with pride at the shop. He was such a cute little tyke. He had made me a present and was so proud as he handed it to me. I was crying and banging my head. I tried to muffle my sounds, so that the children couldn't hear me. I continued to bang my head against the back of the bed. I tried to stop myself but I couldn't. I cried and cried and buried my face in the pillow. Nothing could stop me. I was still crying when Gary walked into the room. He picked me up and tried to shake some sense into me. I rushed into his arms and asked him to help me because I thought I was going insane.

"Please help me, I can't stand the hurt and I can't stop crying."

He could just about make out what I was saying. I was so hysterical. Gary had never seen me this way and he was a little frightened and concerned. He continued to try to knock some sense into me. When that didn't work, he slapped me across the face to jolt me out of my hysteria. I begged him to help me. Gary's face suddenly changed and he looked at me with hatred in his eyes as he said,

"Help you? You killed my son, you bitch. You should never have allowed him to go to the beach. Now I'm going to have to kill you and the kids."

His breathing was labored and his eyes were wild. I tried to free myself from him but he was too strong. He slapped and pushed me down on the floor repeatedly. He was crazy. He raped me, tied me to the bed, tortured me, and beat me for what seemed to be an eternity. I had no fight left in me. I was just like a rag doll. I just lay where he had left me. I didn't even have the strength to cry. He untied me and left. I could hear him sobbing in the bathroom. I did not dare go in to console him. I still cared deeply for this man who had just abused me. When he came out of the bathroom, he came into the bedroom and said,

"I'm no damn good. I'm sick and I want to die."

"Gary, in spite of everything, I still love you and I don't want to lose you. I'd give anything to have you back the way you were before Kevin died."

Gary stiffened at the mention of Kevin's name and he said,

"I will never let myself love again. It's too painful when a loved one is taken away. Please, let me die Melanie, because I'm already dead."

He cried in my arms and he agreed to see a doctor.

"I never wanted to see a doctor before because I always feared the outcome. Now, I don't care. They can put me away if they choose because I believe that I have hurt you enough, dear Melanie."

Time went by and his behavior was still cool with the children. I was afraid to mention the visit to the doctor. I didn't know what his reaction would be. Gary was not being a good father or husband. He paid more attention to his dog. He had become unbearable except for a few moments of tenderness that we shared. He closed down his shop, I wasn't aware of this until I saw him loading the inventory into the shed. Now he had more time to sulk and be insufferable. He was extremely depressed and the children had learned to stay out of his way.

31

One night at the dinner table, Kenny reached for his glass of milk and accidentally dropped it on Gary's lap. That was it! Gary stood up. He seemed to be ten feet tall. He smashed Kenny so hard across the face. He went flying off the chair. Gary then picked up the tablecloth and pulled it so that everything on it went flying into the air. There were broken plates, food, glass, and utensils all over the kitchen floor. I ran to tend to Kenny. Gary grabbed me and threw me across the room. I landed on the stove. Kenny was crying so Gary slapped him and told him to shut up. He slapped him again and again yelling for him to shut up. I jumped on Gary's back and began pulling his hair. He groaned and threw me on the floor. I picked myself up and ran toward him with a broken plate. I screamed and told him that I was going to kill him for having hurt Kenny.

"You can hurt me as you have done so many times, but you can't hurt the children."

I stood before him with the broken plate and said,

"I'm going to kill you if you don't stop and leave Kenny alone."

Suddenly, Gary came to his senses. He looked sadly at me and said,

"Please do. I'll let you."

He started crying and begging me to kill him.

"No," I replied, "you will go to the doctor tomorrow or you will never see us again. I mean it this time Gary. You've gone too far. You're totally out of control when you start taking your anger out on the children. As much as I love you, I won't stand for it. There was no excuse for your outrageous behavior with Kenny tonight. Get to a doctor or we're leaving."

The next day, Gary went to work and made an appointment with the doctor for the following week. During the week he tried very hard to reach the children but they were afraid of him. Gary understood but he still tried. He was gentle and loving with me.

When the day for his scheduled appointment arrived I was excited and nervous. Gary never showed up for dinner. I put the kids to bed. I had some kind of premonition and I didn't want them around when their father came home. I was anticipating something terrible. My heart stopped when I heard the truck pull in the driveway.

Gary never drank during the week. When he came into the house I knew he had been drinking. I should have avoided questioning him about the doctor, but I didn't. He went off into his habitual rage and yelled,

"That's all you care about. You only want me to see a doctor so that he can put me away and you will be rid of me."

He pulled my hair and continued,

"Say it, you bitch, you don't care about my feelings."

He called me every foul name that existed. Karen heard the noise and she came down the stairs. He had me by the throat. She screamed,

"Leave my mother alone."

Gary lunged at her and knocked her to the floor. She lay there very still. Gary looked at her and then at me. He slowly made his way to the door and drove off in his truck.

I took care of Karen and was happy to see she was not too harmed. I woke up the children, told them to dress up, and pack a few things because we were going for a ride in the car. They didn't question me. They did as they were told. We were just about ready to leave when I heard Gary's truck. I told the children to get back into bed and to stay dressed.

"Keep the covers on you and don't make a sound. Keep your shoes on."

They did as they were told and I hid the suitcases.

Gary came in and it was evident that he had had more to drink. He asked me how Karen was. I told him she was fine. I watched him putter around the room. I was on the verge of crying but I was determined to stay calm. I couldn't help but stare at Gary. I thought to myself,

"Damn it, damn it! He looks so normal. "Why can't I reach him? Why doesn't he want to help himself?"

I was so confused. One thing I did know with certainty was that I had to leave him before he severely hurt one of the children. Then maybe he would see a doctor, get better, and we could be a family again. I heard the slamming of the door. Gary had left again. It was my chance.

I didn't waste a minute. I called the children, took the luggage, and quickly left the house. I didn't know where I was going but I drove as fast as I could out of town. I made a few phone calls to my family members. Nobody wanted us. They didn't want to get involved. I was heartsick. I stopped at a motel for the night and put the children to bed.

I was alone with my thoughts. I knew that life as I had known it was over. I had to adjust to living without Gary for the sake of the children. Gary would probably be better off. He might seek help. I secretly hoped for the latter. I had to be firm in my resolution. Maybe my decision would shock him and make him go into some kind of therapy.

I decided to go home the next day when Gary was at work. I'd contact my sister and tell her what had happened and she probably would do something for me. Then I thought of Laurie. I hadn't seen her or Jack in a long time. They probably would help me find a tenement. I could also stay at home and have Gary served. He'd have to move out, but I was too much of a coward to do that.

All of these options raced through my mind. I decided to go home the following day, call my sister, pack as much as I could, and then leave. I decided to write Gary a note.

"Dear Gary, I'm sorry we had to leave you like this. I had no other option. You have become very dangerous lately and you won't do anything about it. I hope our separation is only temporary. It will depend on you. Make an effort and seek professional help. I will be there to help you. It breaks my heart to be separated from you, but there is no other way. I have to think of the beautiful children we've brought into the world. It's not fair to subject them to your fits of insane anger. Please, for our sake, get some help.

Don't be sad and don't be depressed. I'll be back when you say the word. Those words are, *the doctor knows what my problem is and he can help me.* I could never love anyone else as I love you. Take care. Goodbye for now, Gary. All my love forever, Melanie."

I folded the letter, put it into an envelope, and fell asleep.

32

The following day, I called my father-in-law and asked him to come to the house with me because I was afraid to go back alone. Gary might have stayed home from work. He hesitated but I pleaded with him. He finally agreed to let me pick him up. I felt more relaxed knowing that I would not have to face Gary alone. Gary was afraid of his dad.

I stopped for him and headed for home. He didn't have too much to say. Somehow I had managed to keep our problems to ourselves. I told him that I was leaving Gary because he was sick and wouldn't seek any professional help. I also told him that he was beginning to be violent with the children.

"I still love your son dearly, but it's not fair that I subject the children to his rages."

"I don't understand." He said. "Are you sure that you are not inventing this, young lady?"

"Please, believe me. I'm not." I answered. "I won't tell you all of the details now. Maybe sometime later, we can discuss it.'

I started to feel a little hope. If I were to share Gary's bizarre behavior with his parents, maybe they could encourage him to get the help he needed. I was feeling a little remorseful for not having thought about this option before. He would probably welcome their help. I thought it would be the perfect time to talk with Gary and his parents. I felt like kicking myself for not having thought of it before. I had listened to Gary's threats. Every time I mentioned his folks, he threatened to kill me if I did. Now I didn't care because, I knew he wouldn't. He might even be glad for their help. I couldn't wait to get home. Instead of leaving, I would ask Gary's mother and father to come over and I would tell them everything as I should have done a long time ago. I would show him the letter I had written and he would be glad to see me.

When Mr. Daniels and I drove up the driveway we heard a motor running in the garage. I told the children to get back in the car and to stay there. I found Gary's truck in the garage. He had forgotten to shut it off. The fumes were choking me. I was afraid of going to tell Gary about it. He had not left for work yet and it was late. His father pushed me and rushed to the car where Gary was slumped over. He screamed,

"Oh, my God! Don't let me be too late."

Then it hit me. Gary was in the truck. Gary was trying to commit suicide.

"Oh, no! My son!"

Mr. Daniels picked him up and made his way into the house. I still hoped that he was alive. I refused to think differently. When he laid Gary on the couch he cradled him like a child and cried. I knew then that my husband had left me forever. I heard my father-in-law say,

"I didn't know. I didn't know."

He cried for a little while and finally came toward me. I was unable to react. I just kept staring.

"Melanie, did you call an ambulance or the undertaker?"

I didn't answer. I could hear him but I couldn't utter a sound. Everything seemed so far away.

"Melanie, Melanie!" He said as he shook me. "Gary is dead. Do you hear me? He is gone forever."

I nodded, "No...."

He wiped his eyes and told me that he would take care of everything.

I told him that he could do whatever he wanted that I didn't care. Nothing mattered anymore. I went to the couch and laid my head on Gary's body and cried with such despair. I would have given anything to have him back. I was sobbing and shaking Gary's body and telling him to give me another chance. I would not be a coward and I would make sure he got the help he needed. I kept screaming and tugging at his body. I felt two strong hands pulling me by the shoulders to get me off Gary. I fought back. I wanted to die. The doctor and the undertaker tried to comfort me. One of them handed me a glass of water and two pills.

I hadn't even given the children a second thought. Later I found out that they had stayed in the car as I had told them except for Karen. She had seen everything. She did get out of the car. Poor Karen she had witnessed so much violence.

The neighbors were so caring. They helped out and took the children home with them. I watched when they took my husband's body away just as they had carried my son's body. It was too much for me to bear. No one could handle me. The pills did not help. My father-in-law told the doctor that he was very worried. The doctor said,

"I'm worried about Melanie. If she doesn't take control of herself, she can have a heart attack. Losing a husband is hard enough. Having lost a son also, worsens the situation. All we can do is pray that she'll cry herself to sleep and snap out of it. I'll give her something to put her to sleep."

I heard everything that the doctor said, but I could not respond. I didn't care. It was as though I were in a dream. None of this was true. It was just a nightmare. The doctor gave me two more pills and slowly I lost consciousness. The neighbors kept the children and I didn't even care. I slept on Gary's side of the bed and put my head on his pillow. I could smell him and I felt as though he were back in my life. I thought about all the good times that we had had. I minimized the bad ones. My mother-in-law wanted me to stay at her house but I refused to leave because I thought this was just a bad dream and I'd wake up. Gary would come back to me.

33

I had to go to the wake. I knew that it would be painful. I was taken aback when my mother-in-law lost complete control at the funeral home. She cried and begged Gary for forgiveness as she threw herself on his casket.

"Please forgive me, Gary. I know that I should have helped you when you were a child but I was afraid to lose you. You were my only child. I couldn't have loved you more. The doctors gave me such slim odds. You have to understand that I couldn't risk losing you. Do you understand?"

She kept repeating this as she stroked Gary's face and hair. I didn't quite understand what she meant. I knew that I had to help her. I led her away and put my arms around her. We sat silently together and as we cried, she said,

"I have to tell you something, Mel. Even if they rule Gary's death accidental, I know that he committed suicide. Please try to forgive me and understand what I have to tell you."

She told me things that neither Gary nor his father knew.

"Gary's father led a secret life. He married a very nice woman at twenty-three and had three children. He had a great job and seemed to be part of a very happy family. One day on one of his business trips he met me. I had never been married and he courted me. We fell in love. He lied to me. He never told me he was married. He left his wife, his children, and his job. He never saw his family again. I didn't find out about this until much later.

He married me and we started our life together. I was forty years old and Tom was fifty. We were very happy and as old as I was, I desperately wanted a child. I tried for seven years and I thought it was hopeless. Then at forty-eight I became pregnant and nine months later I delivered a beautiful baby boy. I was the happiest person alive. I wore myself out catering to all his needs. As he grew older he was a handful. Tom never helped me with him. I caught Gary taking pleasure in torturing animals. This sent shivers up my spine. I began to believe that he was not normal. I witnessed other odd behavior but I chose to ignore it. I did not want to lose him.

As time went on, there were more incidents and I could not avoid addressing them any more. Without telling my husband, I took Gary to the doctor who ran some tests. Gary had an inoperable brain tumor. The tumor was responsible for his severe headaches and his rages. The doctor told me the chances of a safe operation were very slim. I decided against it. I have lived with this secret all of my life. Now it's too late."

I couldn't hate her because I too, had avoided the truth and done nothing about it. I should have called the psychiatrist the first time Gary had attempted to take his own life. We both had to suffer the consequences of our 'inaction'. We both lost Gary because we didn't have the courage to do what was best for him.

As I gazed on Gary for the last time, I placed a rose on the casket and begged him for forgiveness. I *should* have insisted. I should have made him get medical help.

-34-

The worst wasn't over. I had to bury Gary. Gary's death was ruled accidental, but I knew better. After the funeral I found a letter in Gary's drawer. He must have written it just before he died. I was sure he had put it in the sweater drawer so that I wouldn't find it before the funeral. The note was cold and very matter of fact. An emotionally detached person had written this, not the Gary I thought I knew. It indicated where everything was.

"In my underwear drawer you will find the key to my desk. In the left hand drawer you will find my insurance policies. I have left you financially well off. In the right hand drawer is my bankbook. It contains a lot of cash for you and the family. Don't forget to learn how to balance the checkbook. In the bottom drawer you will find the deed to the house. The house is all paid for. All of the important papers are in this drawer. Don't forget to kiss my dog for me. He's the only one who loved me unconditionally."

This cold note caused me more pain than his death. He said goodbye to his dog and never mentioned his children or me. I cried for the loss of the good times, the bad times, but especially for Gary who had never had a chance at being truly normal.

How I managed to stay sane during the next few months is still a mystery to me. I was pregnant again. I had to cope with so much pain and sorrow and in addition I had to learn how to handle so many legal matters. I didn't understand what

I was doing so I hired a lawyer. He saw how naïve I was, and he took advantage of it. He took a large amount of money for himself. I didn't even care. I had enough money because Gary's death had been ruled accidental. The insurance company paid double indemnity.

As time went by things improved slightly during the day. My nights were unbearable. I kept seeing Gary everywhere. I developed an unhealthy obsession with the afterlife. I wanted to die and be with Gary. The children didn't seem to matter any more. I wasn't eating. I was depressed and absorbed in self-pity. I became a shadow of my former self.

I was so self-centered and concerned about my own pain and problems that I had forgotten about my children and their loss and suffering. I was brought back to the realization that the children were terribly hurt and suffering, when I overheard their conversation one night. Kenny said,

"Is mommy going to die like Kevin and daddy?"

"What's die?" Missy asked.

"I think that mommy doesn't love us any more and she wants to die. She wants to be with daddy and Kevin." Kenny added.

I was so stunned. I had been so selfish. I ran into the room and put my arms around them and told them how much I loved them and that I had been sick but I was feeling better. I promised them that we would be happy again. Kenny asked,

"Does that mean that my daddy is going to come back?"

I couldn't handle it. I ran out of the room crying. I knew that Karen would handle the situation and answer the question. What a blessing she was.

That night, I sat down and made plans for the future. I had promised the children a better future and I would deliver on that promise. I finally decided to look for another house. I thought that the move would alleviate some of the pain and hurt caused by too many sad memories.

The following day I went to visit Laurie to tell her about my plans. I took the kids with me and they were delighted to get out of the house. I knew that she was home because I had called before. The children were so happy to see her family. They went off and played together. I sat down for coffee and told Laurie about my plans to buy a house. It would have to be near the farm because I had no intention of selling Gary's house.

"I'm hoping that I'll be able to return there someday. Someday when the memories are not so fresh."

I started to cry. Laurie who wanted to change the subject quickly said,

"Mel, there's a cute little cape for sale on the other street. It would be wonderful to have you so close. It's only five minutes away from your farm."

"Let's go see it." I said.

For the first time in a long time I was excited. It was much smaller than I had anticipated but it was nice. I really didn't care what I bought. This house would be ideal for me because I would be close to my friends. That night I closed the deal. I met with the real estate agent and paid cash. I really made a good buy. Thank God that Jack had come with me. He helped with the paper work and made me realize I had made a good purchase.

The children were so excited when I told them about my decision. I didn't think they'd react that way. We were beginning a new chapter of our lives. Hopefully, it would be a happy one.

35

I bought new furniture for the new house. I even bought myself a new bedroom set. I really didn't want to disturb anything in the old house. I was leaving everything the way it had been when Gary was alive. I didn't know why. When I was settled in, I knew I had made the correct decision for the moment. The children adjusted very well. We lived on a dead end street. That meant they could ride their bicycles in the road. There were dozens of children with whom they played. Doreen volunteered to care for my children if I had to run some errands.

She was Laurie's next-door neighbor and she had five children of her own. At first, I was afraid of imposing on her, but Laurie convinced me that Doreen really loved children and she wanted to take care of them. I agreed on the condition she let me pay for the service. She refused to accept money but she had no choice, I just left it on the table as I walked out of her house.

I had no conception of the value of money. I knew I had plenty of it and I bought what I wanted when I wanted. I didn't even think of the future.

One Tuesday, I asked Doreen to baby-sit for me because I had a doctor's appointment. Naturally she agreed. I was much bigger than I had been for my previous pregnancies. I was convinced it was because I had lost so much weight in the past months so the baby showed more prominently. I was wrong, the doctor told me that I was having twins. I almost passed out.

"Are you sure?"

"Definitely! There are two heartbeats. I can arrange to have x-rays taken if you wish."

"No, I'm sure that you are right." I answered.

I was too numb to know how I felt. I wasn't going to tell anyone, but when I got to Doreen's house and she asked me how I was, I blurted out,

"I'm going to have twins."

Her enthusiasm and happiness helped me feel better.

"Don't worry about it. I will help you as much as I can."

I knew she meant it. I left and tried to go on with my life as best as I could. I visited the farm every now and then. Sometimes Laurie would come with me and on a few occasions I brought Doreen.

Doreen had a great time going through all the 'stuff' that Gary and I had accumulated. What I called junk she called treasures. She went to the shed and discovered an intercom system that Gary had not installed because of some electrical problem. She asked if she could have her husband look at it because he was handy with electrical gadgets. I told her that she could have and take anything she wanted because I didn't want any of the things in the shed. She told me I was crazy and that I should have a huge yard sale. I could make a lot of money.

"Not now," I answered. "I'm not interested."

The summer went by quickly and I was beginning to be able to smile. I was surrounded by caring people. They kept the children and me occupied. I became much closer to Laurie and started to confide in her. I knew that her husband Jack liked me too. I felt welcomed when I visited her. It was great to be at ease with someone. I was able to talk to Laurie. We talked about almost everything. I did leave some embarrassing things out. I think it would have been too hard for her to believe some of those things. Later, I would tell her *all* about my life.

Seven and half months after Gary's death, I gave birth to twins, two girls. It was a difficult birth because the babies were so big. The doctor had to use forceps. I tried but I couldn't be completely happy. I missed my long stemmed rose. The memory of Gary and Kevin's loss was still painful. It wasn't fair. Why was I able to have all those children and not be allowed to have a father to take care of them? I felt cheated. It just wasn't fair. I was feeling sorry for myself and I had worked myself into a crying session when Laurie walked into the room.

"Don't cry Mel, Try to be happy. Your twins are beautiful. Be patient. Things will soon improve. Time heals all wounds."

I knew that she was right. I told her the story of the rose and that was the reason I was crying. She told me to be courageous and that I now had 'six' reasons for trying to put my life together again.

It took time but luckily, I had a great support system. I had so many friends who were always there to help. My sister came to visit me and she stayed for a few days. I enjoyed her company and she was a great help and comfort to me.

Laurie's visits were more frequent and I told her all the intimate details of my life with Gary. I didn't leave anything out.

"Enough of that! You're making me jealous." Laurie said in jest. "You certainly were the x-rated couple of the year."

She told me that what Gary and I had shared sexually was rare and I'd always have the memories. She also told me to write my memoirs.

"Write it, Melanie."

"You write it, Laurie."

Laurie said she was only kidding and that she didn't know anything about writing.

"There's always a first time." I replied.

36

I was comfortable in my new neighborhood but I was too cramped. The house was too small for such a large family. It was cluttered with kids, high chairs, and toys. I missed my old house. I started spending more time over there until I decided to go back. I felt strong enough to handle the move. The children were upset but I knew they would adjust. The farm was a much better place for them and they had never been without friends. I told Laurie and Jack of my plans and they agreed to help me. Doreen and her husband and my other friends also helped me pack and move.

Once we were in the house, Doreen helped me put things into place and her husband installed the intercom system he had repaired. They were such a nice couple. They took the time to help me when they had so much work of their own. They were so lucky. They had each other and their five children. I started feeling sorry, but I caught myself and tried to be happy with what I had.

Once I had moved back, I got myself into a routine. I made friends with the neighbors. One of them was an older lady who lived alone. Another one was a divorcee whose husband had left for another woman. She kept asking me to go with her to the nightclub but I kept putting her off.

I was very fortunate, I didn't lack for baby-sitters. Doreen would take care of the children during the day if I needed to go on an errand. Mrs. Lancaster would stay with the children at night if I needed her. She said it was a great distraction for her. She lived all alone and it could be very lonely. I thought I was very lucky to find someone to stay with six children. I know that I paid them well, but you can't buy peace of mind and that's what they provided.

I still spent a great deal of time with Laurie. She was my best friend. I could discuss any problem with her. We became amateur psychologists and tried to analyze my life before I married Gary and Gary's life and problems. We came up with some good reasons for certain behaviors and possible solutions to problems. It was therapeutic to talk about the past and we enjoyed it. We made a game of it.

"Still think that my life would be the subject of a good book?" I asked.

"Yes, I do. I wouldn't know how to go about it. Only professional people are successful." Laurie replied.

I asked Laurie what she thought about my going out with Sylvia. She told me I should get out and begin to socialize. Then she told me about her brother's band.

"You're going out with Jack and me, Doreen and Paul, Rita and George, and Carol and Bob next Saturday night. My brother plays the organ, the sax, and he sings. We'll pick you up at seven o'clock and bring you back home after the dance."

Laurie was right. I had a great time and her brother's band was very good. The place was jumping all night. Everybody took turns and asked me to dance. I liked her single brother Nick. He took me home and was a real gentleman. We talked for a long period of time and I knew that we had formed a brother/sister relationship. I met him many times after that because I continued to go with the 'gang' every Friday night.

I couldn't put Sylvia off any longer. I decided to accept her invitation to go to the nightclub. I felt uncomfortable walking into the club but once I sat down I started to relax and enjoy the music. I danced with a few men but one man in particular kept coming back and I thought that he was handsome. I danced with him the rest of the night. He asked me all kinds of questions about myself. Stupidly, I told him I was a widow and that I lived alone. I naively told him how old I was and where I lived. I didn't think there was anything wrong with my responses until I got into the car and Sylvie yelled at me,

"Are you crazy? You just don't go around telling strangers that you live alone, especially when you live in the woods. You never know what could happen to you."

Oh, well," I shrugged. "Next time I won't."

When I got home, I thanked Mrs. Lancaster and got ready for bed. I heard a loud noise in the woods behind my house. I heard something near the window. I was terrified. I went to the front door to make sure the chain was on the door. It wasn't. As I was putting the hook on, the doorknob turned. I had forgotten to lock the door. Luckily the latch was still on. I came face to face with a stranger. I screamed hysterically but he still tried to come in. I dialed my neighbor's number and asked him to please come to help me. In a matter of seconds, he was in the driveway and had grabbed the kid by the neck.

His wife must have called the police because they were there in a matter of minutes.

The young man had seen me at the club, and followed me home. He was looking for someone he knew, he said. He must have gone to the wrong house.

"Liar," I screamed, "you saw me and you heard me screaming, but you still tried to force your way in. I'm pressing charges."

The following day, the police came over with a lame story. They told me that the kid was on leave from the service and he came from a good family. The police added that he was drunk at the time. He really thought he was at his friend's house. They obviously knew him and they wanted me to drop the charges. I agreed.

Two weeks later, I went out with Sylvia again. I walked into a club in town and I saw this gorgeous man. Our eyes met and I began shaking inside. I hadn't felt like this since Gary had died. If I had had any sense I would have run out of the place.

"Talk about chemistry " He said

What?" I had not heard what he said.

"Hi! My name is Bruce. Talk about chemistry." He said. "I know you felt it too."

I hadn't even taken my seat yet, and I was in his arms dancing. We didn't even speak. After the dance he thanked me, led me to my seat, and walked away.

"Wow! What was that all about?" Asked Sylvia.

"I don't know but it scares me. I don't like the feelings he brings up in me. I had those same feelings with Gary and I became his sex slave. Gary had such a hold on me. I couldn't resist him. I don't want the same thing to happen to me again. Once in a life time is more than enough, thank you!"

"Gee," Sylvia said, "what an exciting love life you must have had. It sounds as though it was great. Mine was lousy. All he ever thought of was his own satisfaction."

"Well, as fantastic as mine was, I couldn't handle another one like it." I responded.

Sylvia looked puzzled but I didn't bother to explain. Bruce asked me for the next dance. I snuggled in his arms and forgot what I had just told Sylvia. He was a wonderful dancer and a smooth talker. He asked me if I would go to dinner with him some evening. I told him I would think about it. He didn't like my answer but he didn't comment.

I couldn't wait to tell Laurie all about my evening. I asked her if she thought that I should accept Bruce's invitation.

"Not yet, Mel, you just met him. If you feel so helpless in his presence, maybe it would be wise to avoid him completely. You might be getting involved in the same way you were with Gary. Then it will be too late to leave him. I can't really tell you what to do. You're the one that experiences those feelings. You told me that you didn't want to go back to being a sex slave. I don't know what a sex slave is. I never had first hand experience, but it sounds exciting and also very dangerous. You make the decision. I can only advise you. I just did."

I listened to her and I knew she was right. Bruce must have gotten my telephone number from someone at the club because he kept calling me up for a date. I kept putting him off and gave all kinds of excuses. There was something in the tone of his voice that made me leery but I didn't quite know what it was. As usual I didn't listen to reason and I went with my feelings. I saw him again at the club and danced with him all night. I knew I was falling in love with him but I was cautious and I kept him at a distance. I could tell by his expression that he was losing patience. I noticed that he perspired profusely if he was tense. I once again took the blame. It was my fault. I was too distant. I was toying with him. What a loser I was!

38

The twins were growing. They were happy babies and the rest of the children seemed to be adjusting to their new surroundings. One night during the late evening I received a disturbing phone call. It was an anonymous call from a pervert. He whispered in a guttural voice all kinds of obscenities.

"I'm going to get you. I'm going toxxxxxxx."

I was extremely upset. The phone calls continued. Whoever it was knew my name. I called the operator and asked her not to let the calls through, but she couldn't do anything about it.

I continued to get the same kind of calls all week. The voice and the content of those calls scared me to death. I had nightmares that terrified me. Finally, I had my phone number changed and the calls stopped.

While I was dancing with Bruce the following weekend, I told him about the phone call incidents. He seemed concerned and said,

"Mel, you shouldn't live alone in that big house. It's dangerous. You should let me take you out and take care of you. You can resist me as long as you want, but you are destined to be mine."

That statement sent an all out systems alert to my mind and it reminded me of the control Gary had had over me. I didn't think Bruce was sick, but I did think he was possessive and controlling. I forgot all about common sense when he held me close as we danced and he whispered that he loved me and

I had to be his. We hadn't ever been on a date and here he was telling me that he loved me. I didn't know what to do. I could feel myself falling in love or was it lust with him.

I wanted to go home. I was going to try to forget him. He kissed me goodnight and all of the old desires came back to me. I wanted to stay, but I broke away and ran to my car. He didn't have my new phone number so he couldn't call me.

Once again, I went to see my faithful friend Laurie for advice. I told her about the meeting with Bruce, about my ambivalent feelings, and about my decision. She said,

"Let's analyze this objectively. Why do you want to leave him?'

"I don't feel that I can handle the commitment right now. I'm not ready for marriage. I don't want to see him again because I don't think I will have the strength to resist him. He would be as good a lover as Gary was when he was normal. Part of me wants that and another part of me is saying:

"Cool it girl! I don't want to be anyone's sex slave again. I let Gary use me and I won't let it happen again. I want to be my own person. I know my weaknesses. I have to avoid Bruce. I'm sure he's no good for me."

"If that's the way you feel then by all means stay away from him. I give you credit for doing the right thing. I hope you can follow through with your decision." Laurie added.

39

I was determined to be firm in my decision. I was happy I was not receiving any more harassing phone calls. Many nights I would sit in the family room after the children were in bed and I'd have a pity party. I would think of Bruce and our last kiss. I would reminisce about Gary and my love life and let myself feel the passion that I had felt, and then I'd work myself into a crying frenzy.

On one of those nights, I heard a terrible noise in the woods. It sounded like crashing bottles. I ran to the door to make sure that all the doors were locked. I heard another crash and footsteps outside my door. I called on my neighbor Frank to come and check the yard for me. Before he came, I heard a banging at the window. We checked everywhere in the yard and saw nothing. The police checked and found nothing.

The following day, I went out into the yard because I was certain I had heard something. I had not imagined it. I found a pile of broken bottles next to the stone wall. The police came to check and told me that they would patrol the area more closely. The same thing happened the following two nights. I thought I would go crazy. I called up Laurie and told her about all of the strange happenings. I told her that I was afraid of staying alone.

"Look Mel, pack up the things that you need and come on over with the kids until we can figure out what to do." Laurie suggested.

"Thanks Laurie, I couldn't do that. That's too much."

"I don't want to hear another word. You know that Jack and I don't mind. We'll have fun. We'll make a party out of this."

I moved in with Laurie and Jack and their five kids. There were fourteen of us. What a family! It was hectic at times, but most of the time it was enjoyable. We followed a good routine. Jack was so giving. The children and I felt welcomed and we were grateful.

Doreen was great help. She came over and took some of the kids to her house, fed them and kept them overnight. I decided to call the lawyers, the local police, and the state police. They all said the same thing. They could do nothing except keep a closer watch on the property until they caught the culprit.

Meanwhile Laurie and I continued our conversations until the wee hours of the morning. She really cared about me and she enjoyed our conversations about Gary and my tormented life. She really helped me and made me realize so many things about myself that would hopefully help me to face the future. I knew I would eventually have to move back home and I dreaded it. I wished I had not sold my little cape. I had never been frightened before, but I was then.

Laurie's brother, Nick, had been coming over for coffee quite often. He was working in the area and he'd drop by on his coffee break. He was aware of my situation and he offered a possible solution.

"If you agree Mel, I'll come over at night and sleep on the couch. No strings attached. I won't bother you as long as you make my lunch just like my mother does. When I have a date you can have one of your friends stay with you until I come home."

"What a good idea!" Said Laurie.

I agreed and Nick moved in. I really enjoyed his company and we would talk for hours. He was never anything more than a big brother to me. People were talking but we knew the truth and didn't care about public gossip.

Nick stayed with me for two weeks. Finally we decided I was strong enough to stay by myself. One night I went out with Laurie and her friends. When we got to the club, to my astonishment, Bruce was at the bar. I wanted to turn around and leave but secretly I had missed him terribly and tried to forget him, but I kept thinking about him and wondering how he was. I had almost succumbed and gone to the bar to accidentally 'bump' into him. Now I was facing him. He just stared at me and said nothing. I felt hurt but I couldn't blame him. I had treated him quite shabbily.

Someone asked to dance and I accepted. Then Bruce grabbed my arm and said that I was with him. I felt embarrassed. Bruce put his arms around me and asked me how I was. He continued,

"I've missed you very much, but I knew we would meet again. You can just put me off for so long. Someday I'll break you. I love you and I'll wait."

I didn't' say anything. I couldn't. I felt so right in his arms. After the dance I went back to the table and introduced him. He was polite but shy. I asked Laurie if she minded if I went home with Bruce. She said,

"It's your life, Melanie. It looks like he's finally won."

40

We left early and drove up to my driveway. I was surprised that he knew where I lived. I didn't give it another thought. Maybe I should have. He was a smooth operator. He knew what to say and when to say it. I was so taken up with him that I would have given him anything he wanted, but he didn't press me for anything. I just kissed him lightly and said goodnight. I gave him my phone number so that he could get in touch with me.

I had just started undressing when the phone rang. I froze.

"Not again!"

It was Bruce telling me he loved me. He just wanted to hear my voice. He asked me if I loved him. I told him it was too soon.

The following day, Laurie came over and she didn't mince any words. She told me there was something about Bruce that made her suspicious. I should not marry him. If I did it would be a terrible mistake.

"I don't know what it is, but I was watching him all night and I don't like the way he stared at you. I don't know what it is but there's something wrong with him. I'm sorry you asked me. I've only seen him once. I know that you're 'hooked' on him and I do hope I'm wrong. I pray to God that he doesn't hurt you the same way Gary did.

I told Laurie about our little episode in the car. She didn't quite understand the part that he had refused to make love. Then she told me he was toying with me.

"He wanted to impress you. He wanted you to believe he was a nice guy and not taking advantage of you on the first night."

I kind of accepted that explanation but it didn't account for the fact that he always seemed to avoid every opportunity to be intimate. He had me climbing the walls.

One night we were alone in the den. He had every opportunity to make love to me in the privacy of my home and once again, after letting himself and me get to a point of wild passion, he pulled away and just sat there. He stared blankly at me, breathing heavily. Great beads of sweat poured down his forehead. He got up and left. Laurie and I couldn't figure it out. We thought that he had a physical problem.

"Why don't you come right out and ask him?"

Laurie said to me during one of our conversations.

I did ask him. He said there was nothing wrong with him. He just didn't think it was the appropriate time for lovemaking. I didn't understand and neither did Laurie.

Late one night I heard the breaking of bottles again. Not again! Laurie and Doreen showed up and stayed the night. We had a good time and once again Laurie said,

"Boy! That would be another good chapter in your book."

"Did you start it yet?" I asked her

"I'm not kidding Mel. Let's face it your life is unbelievable. If I hadn't witnessed most of it I would doubt some parts. I have jotted down a few notes here and there. Maybe some day..."Laurie added and I laughed.

The evening went by quickly. What good husbands they both had. I was worried because they had been out so late. They laughed and Laurie said,

"They won't even know what time it is because they'll be sound asleep. Doreen and I do this often. Either she comes over my house to play scrabble or I go over to hers to play cards. Our husbands don't mind as long as we don't disturb their sleep. So don't worry your pretty little head."

The same kind of vandalism happened three times that week. I couldn't call on Doreen and Laurie constantly. Whoever wanted to scare me was doing a terrific job. It was always the same pattern, the breaking of bottles followed by the sound of footsteps. Somehow the perpetrator managed to escape without getting caught. I never heard a car or a truck driving off. The police had no clue either.

Later that week I went to dinner with Bruce and told him about my problem. He seemed genuinely concerned and he offered the same solution as before,

"Marry me and I bet that you'll never be frightened again."

"Why would you want to marry me? You hardly know me and I have six kids. You're not even working. You're still laid off from work aren't you?"

"Just for a little while longer. They're calling me back very soon. I want to marry you because I love you. I told you that from the very beginning and I wasn't kidding when I said it. I meant every word I said. You are going to be mine forever. How about it? Marry me and you won't be afraid any more."

41

When Bruce drove me home that night, he followed me in. We sat in the den on the couch. We talked for a while. I noticed that he was perspiring and he kissed me softly. Then all hell broke loose. He broke all records. He was a little too rough even for me. We both acted like love-starved animals. I finally had to snap him back to reality. I couldn't take any more. It was the first time I made love since Gary's death. I had mixed emotions of joy and guilt. What a fool I was to fall in love with someone who was just like Gary. He asked me if he could stay the night and I couldn't refuse him. I didn't like the look on his face. It was tense and pensive, but I let him stay anyhow.

The following day, I was telling Laurie about it and she said,

"I don't know Mel, there's something strange about him. I don't like it. Did you accept his marriage proposal yet?

"No, I didn't give him an answer. I want to marry him because I love him and I wouldn't have to be frightened anymore, but for some reason I'm afraid to take the next step."

"Then don't do it!" Laurie said.

I told Laurie that when I had sex with Bruce it had been very painful. I felt as if I had a lump in my pelvic area. She told me to get to the doctor quickly. I called the doctor and he gave me an appointment immediately. Laurie took care of the children for me.

When I came back I told her that it was nothing serious. The doctor had taken care of it in the office. It was painful but I was relieved to know that it was nothing serious.

That night there was a repeat performance of vandalism. I lost control opened the door and ran into the night screaming,

"Who are you? What do you want? Answer me."

I finally got a hold of myself and went into the house. I called Bruce but there was no answer. I didn't want to call the police because I was sure that by now they had me pegged as a 'nut' case. I just curled up on the couch and cried like a baby. When I was seemingly calm I tried to read, but I couldn't get interested. I sat there waiting for something tragic to happen.

The phone rang and it was Bruce. I was so glad to hear a familiar voice. I started to cry. He told me to control myself and he'd be right over.

"Melanie, if you're so damned scared, why don't you do something about it? I told you that I want to marry you. If you love me why are you holding back? It's as though you want to punish me for something. Maybe that's why your husband beat you up. You probably teased the hell out of him and drove him to it."

His comments stopped me from crying. I didn't say a word. I forgot them when he came over and took me into his arms. He turned me into a lamb. He was so gentle as he prepared me for lovemaking. I noticed that he wanted to be rough but he restrained himself. I was almost sorry because some of my best love sessions with Gary had been wild and rough. Bruce held back and this caused him to tense up and form beads of sweat on his forehead.

42

Once again I approached Laurie with my problem. I asked her if she thought it was a good idea to marry Bruce. She quickly said,

"Don't. I don't like that man. You're not going to be happy. He already thinks he owns you. He doesn't have a decent job. He's extremely jealous and he doesn't like your friends. He especially hates me."

I interrupted.

"That's because I told him you didn't like him. I'm sorry. That's why he wants me to avoid you."

"Mel, I know he's gorgeous and he's a great lover, but those are not sufficient reasons. I think you will be making a big mistake if you marry him. I could be wrong but.." Laurie said.

"Well, even if I had doubts, it's too late. I think that I'm pregnant." I told her.

"Please don't tell anyone. I haven't told a soul. I am sure that I love him. I am going to take a chance."

"I wish you well Mel, if you ever need me I'll be available. "Laurie said.

She was teary eyed because she knew that she wouldn't be seeing much of me after I married Bruce. I didn't say anything to Laurie but Bruce didn't want me to have anything to do with her at all. He didn't mind Doreen because she was still baby-sitting the children.

After I left Laurie, I went over to Doreen's and told her that I was getting married. She congratulated me and I showed her my diamond ring. I hadn't shown it to Laurie. I had paid for it but Bruce said that it was only a loan and he would repay me. I asked Doreen if she would take care of the children while we were on our honeymoon. She was happy to do so.

"I'll make arrangements and I'll let you know how many of the children you will have. You will definitely have the twins. Guess where we are going on our honeymoon? Bruce wants us to go to Las Vegas,"

"Who's paying?" She asked.

"Well, I am but it's only a loan. I've always wanted to travel and I've got the money. So why not?"

We were married in a small private ceremony. I didn't invite Laurie or Doreen. We flew to Las Vegas and I quickly had to face reality. Bruce was very moody and he left me by myself quite often. He was frequently looking up names in the directory. When I asked him what he was doing he answered 'nothing'. So I didn't probe. Most of the time he was a good lover but sometimes he frightened me. He left me with a strange cold feeling that I could not explain.

He was an enigma and I couldn't figure him out. I did not know the man he became. I hardly knew the man that he had been. Maybe I had never known who he really was. There was something strange and scary about the way he acted, the way he looked, and the way he breathed. There was something there that I didn't understand. He loved to spend money – mine! We spent five thousand dollars in Las Vegas. He wanted to rent the best cars; dine at the most extravagant restaurants; gamble at the casinos; buy the most extravagant clothes and gifts; and stay at the best hotels. In two weeks all of the five thousand dollars was gone.

Very shortly after our return I became disillusioned and realized that my husband was not the man that I thought he was. I had known he was demanding and possessive, and now I knew he was also a spender of my money and a liar.

43

Not long after our honeymoon a young woman came to the house. When Bruce saw her, all the blood drained from his face. She said,

"I came back to get my car, you cad. I just found out you got married. Why didn't you have the decency to tell me?"

She turned around, looked at me and continued,

"Sister, I feel sorry for you. You married the biggest loser ever. He's nothing but a user, a liar, and a taker."

She turned around and told him,

"Give me my keys, you bastard."

Bruce lunged toward her and shoved her out of the door. I had never seen him so angry. He looked like a madman. He scared me. I don't know what they said to each other but I overheard her say,

"I'll come back with the cops."

Whatever else she said was effective because she drove off with the car.

"I want an explanation." I demanded.

He still had that crazed look, so I wasn't too brave.

"Don't you demand anything from me, if you know what's good for you!"

I knew well enough to keep quiet. He was acting like a maniac. He kicked the hell out of the poor dog, broke the cupboard door, and threw the glassware on the floor. I just stayed out of his way. Thank God the children were not in the house.

When he had calmed down, he told me that he had bought the car before he met me. He made the mistake of letting her register it in her name, so he had no claim on it.

"I just assumed that the car was still mine because I had paid for it."

I didn't believe him, but far be it for me to tell him.

Bruce finally went back to work after a few months. I was so glad to get him out of the house during the day. I bought him a new truck for which I paid cash. He loved it. He was like a little kid. He had expensive tastes. He always came home with new and name brand clothes.

I hadn't seen Laurie since my marriage. Now that Bruce was back at work, I could go visit her. She was happy to see me. She asked me how things were. I answered,

"Not so good."

I surprised myself with that statement, but it was the truth.

"Bruce is a very selfish person. He's mean and doesn't care about the kids. He just likes the twins.

"What about you? You don't look very pregnant. She asked.

"It was a false alarm."

"That's good. Be careful. Don't take any chances of becoming pregnant."

I wasn't going to say anything but Laurie had a way of getting me to confide in her. So I told her there was no way I could make my husband change the way he made love to me. He was a sadist and a pervert. I knew I was using the proper term because I had looked it up in the dictionary. He had hidden his true character before we were married. I sensed there was something the matter with him.

"I was too stupid to listen to my intuition or to you for that matter. He takes pleasure in torturing me."

Laurie interrupted my thoughts.

"I don't want to hear any more Melanie, until you decide to do something about it. What are you going to do?"

"Nothing," I said, "He pushed me into a wall the other day and told me that he would not allow me to ever, ever leave him. He meant it and I'm afraid for me and for the children."

It was the past revisited. Bruce used the same words and threats that Gary had used. How could I fall into the same trap twice? I had had two sick husbands. I must have been the sick one. I seemed to attract perverted men and I loved them.

"I shared tender moments with Gary, but Bruce is always brutal and he doesn't have a tender fiber in his body. He's a liar, a cheat, and a thief. Gary had a sickness, but Bruce is not human"

Laurie interrupted,

"Why don't you leave him, you jerk?"

"Because I'm afraid to die. He means what he is saying."

"Oh, he's full of crap."

"That's what I thought about Gary too, and he carried out his threats when I left him." I said.

"What can I say?" Replied Laurie.

44

Things got progressively worse at home. I was ashamed to go see Laurie so I avoided her. I knew I was wrong to stay with Bruce but I didn't have the courage to leave him. On occasion, Bruce would be nice to me. Most of the time he lied.

He was sneaky and stole all kinds of things from me. I noticed that many of Gary's tools and equipment were disappearing from the garage and the shed. That was where Gary kept his power tools and the inventory from his business. One day I confronted Bruce. He looked at me straight in the eye and told me he would be on the lookout for the robber. I suspected my husband because everything was under lock and key and there was no evidence of a break-in.

He was so stupid. He could have asked me for anything and I would have given it to him. One night when he was at his habitual hangout, the corner bar, one of his friends came over to the house. He asked me to tell Bruce that he needed to exchange some of the plugs and windshield wipers he had bought from him. I told him he'd have to talk to Bruce and he was at the bar.

"Call before you come because he stays out late." I told him.

"That's where my things are going. Bruce is selling them and pocketing the money." I said to myself.

When Bruce came home, I was sound asleep. I waited for the following night before mentioning anything. I told him that he was nothing but a crook. He turned into a demented demon. He beat and tortured me, and succeeded in breaking my fingers. The animal left me on the floor cringing in agony. He stormed out of the house as he slammed the door. I left the children and made my way to the police station. It wasn't the first time that I had been there. I had previously reported Bruce for assault and battery. Another time I had gone there with a broken nose. This time I was there with a bleeding face and broken fingers. One of the policemen wanted to take me to the hospital.

"Not right now," I said, "I want to press charges."

"Lady, all we can do is warn him to leave you alone. Unless you press charges and serve him with restraining papers, we can't do much else. After he is served with the order, we'll make sure he doesn't go near your house." They told me.

"I'll think about it." I said.

Then, I let him take me to the hospital. My fingers healed, but not the pain in my heart. I found out later that the police had visited my husband at the bar. They told him to leave me alone. He told them to mind their own business.

"She's my wife and I'll treat her the way that I want to. What do you know about it? She deserves what she gets. You don't know what kind of wife she really is. So butt out."

"Don't get wise punk. We've got a name for people like you. If you don't watch your step, we'll make sure you get yours." The police told him as they walked away.

Bruce never mentioned this incident to me. Someone who had been at the bar when the policemen paid him a 'visit' told me about it. The policeman didn't frighten him. He didn't alter his behavior at all.

One night when Bruce was at the bar, I decided to get a baby-sitter and I went shopping. When I got home he had sent the baby-sitter home and was waiting for me.

"Where have you been you tramp?"

He continued to berate me with the vilest, filthiest words. I did not know what half of them meant. This was something that Gary had never done. THE LIGHT went on...I suddenly realized that I recognized the words and the voice. He was the O-N-E who had called me on the phone before I was married. He was the one who had made all the noise with the bottles in the woods. This knowledge frightened me beyond anything that I had experienced. He had tricked me into marrying him for protection. I was so ashamed and disgusted with myself and with him. I was even more outraged that he had made me an accomplice in his perverted and depraved behavior. I didn't say anything.

I knew I was in for a rough night. I decided that I would rather die than continue this charade for the rest of my life. I would leave when he was at work.

The following day, I called Laurie, but she wasn't home. I left a message with Jack I told him it was urgent for Laurie to get in touch with me.

-45-

The rest of this novel is narrated by Laurie Casey.

When I got home Jack said to me,
"Laurie, Melanie called. I never tell you what to do, but you really should *not* call her back right now. I'm worried that you are getting too involved. We have done all that we can for her."

I really wanted to call her, but I listened to my husband. I told Doreen about it and she agreed with Jack. We should stay out of Melanie's life.

"You know that Bruce doesn't like you. If you call and he is home it might make things more difficult for her." Doreen said.

Two weeks later, Melanie called me.

"I called you two weeks ago. I guess you didn't get my message or you just didn't want to talk to me."

She was smart enough to guess the truth. I didn't want her to feel rejected, so I told her a white lie. I told her I hadn't gotten the message.

"You are going to be proud of me!" She continued. "I have left my husband and I have retained a lawyer. He's working on the documents to have him served. May I come over and talk to you?"

"Sure," I answered, "bring the kids over. I haven't seen them in a long time."

I decided to take some chicken out of the freezer because I wanted to invite them for dinner. As I waited for their arrival I started thinking about all the things that had happened to her. I felt badly for her. She always seemed to be the recipient of tragic events. Even when she was happy she seemed to be so melancholic. She had sad brown eyes like those of a wounded doe.

I should have told her what Doreen had found out about Bruce. He had been married before. He used to beat his first wife and his two kids. She feared him so much she took the two kids and fled to Las Vegas. She changed her name and left no forwarding address. That was why he wanted to go to Las Vegas for his honeymoon. I decided not to share that information with Melanie just yet. She had enough problems.

Melanie came to see me with the children. I thought I had seen the last of her and her problems. I couldn't ignore her. I cared too much. I had to try to help once again. She sat down and we had coffee. The children were amusing themselves with my kids. She shed a few tears and proceeded to tell me all the horrible details of her relationship with Bruce. They were so gory and frightening. I thought that I had heard it all with her tales about Gary. In comparison, they were quite mild. Her life with Bruce was pure hell.

"What the hell attracts you to men like that? I know they're good-looking but..." I asked.

"I really don't know. All I know is that it's over and I am not going to change my mind. I am going to leave him." She answered.

"You mean you're still with him?' I almost screamed.

"I have no choice until he gets served. I'm petrified of him. I won't tell him anything until he gets the restraining order. I have to wait. There's nothing else I can do. He won't agree to a separation. I have to make a new life for the children and me. If he has any inkling of what I am about to do, he'll beat the children and me."

"Then you can't possible stay for dinner?" I said.

"No, thank you. I don't dare. I don't want to anger him."

Friday of that week she called to tell me that Bruce was being served on that day. She told me she was so nervous. I invited her to come over the house and she accepted. As we talked she inquired about my friends. I asked her to come with me to the club that night. She liked the idea of seeing everyone again. She asked me about Nick and I told her that he was fine.

As she was leaving, she put her hand on my son's face and remarked how like her Kevin he was. She then kissed his forehead. I don't know what it was about this girl but I always felt so sad for her.

When we went to the club that evening, we were three couples in my car. This included my brother and his wife, Doreen and her husband, and Jack and me. We drove by the farm to pick up Melanie. She was ready and very jittery. I whispered to her and asked her if she had heard from Bruce.

"Not a word". She said.

"Good!" I answered. "Maybe he'll realize that you mean business."

"I hope so." She said.

We had a good time. Melanie seemed to be enjoying herself. I noticed that she was drinking a little more than usual. We all were, but none of us was drunk. We were just happy and certainly feeling no pain. Melanie was sitting next to me and telling me about her plans for the future.

"No more men in my future. I am going to concentrate on the children and myself.

"The hell with men. Who needs them."

She went on and on.

"Good for you." I agreed.

"Bruce meant it when he said that he would never let me go. He would see me dead before I left him. He said it very often when he was hurting me. "She said.

"Mel," I added, "he's only saying that because he's a coward and insecure. He knows how gullible you are and how easily you can be taken advantage of. He knows he can scare you into staying with him. Don't think of those things any more. Look ahead to a brighter future." I said.

"You are right, my friend. Look ahead and not back." She laughed.

She got up and danced with my brother. Later on, she whispered into my ear that she was foolish, but she still loved Bruce.

"But I'll never go back to him."

"Go dance, you crazy idiot. You don't know what love is." I replied.

I was busy having a good time and then I noticed that Melanie was not around. I asked my brother where she was and he told me she had a little too much to drink and that he had put her in his car and locked the doors so she could sleep. I probably would have gone to check on her myself but I was not too steady on my feet myself. I kept on dancing until it was time to go home. After the dance, we were all in the parking lot and I went to check on Melanie. I knocked on the window and she woke up.

"How do you feel?" I asked.

"Good, I got rid of my headache. Nick gave me two aspirins. Now I feel fine."

I asked her if she was coming home with us and Nick said that he would take her home after they went for coffee. I kissed her and gave her a hug. She said,

"Thank you, Laurie for being my friend."

She hung on to me for a second and I said,

"Hey, my sad little friend, no more sadness, and that's an order. Be happy!"

46

The next morning, my brother Dave, the sax player called. He asked me if I had taken Melanie home from the dance. I told him that Nick had.

"Why do you want to know?" I asked.

He said he had just received a strange phone call.

"I think that it was a cop. He was asking me all kinds of questions about Melanie. I didn't have any answers, and he wouldn't tell why he was calling."

I felt horrible. I knew that something was terribly wrong. I immediately hung up the phone and called Nick. My mother answered and told me Nick was still sleeping. I told her to wake him up. It was terribly important.

"What's up?" He asked sleepily.

"What did you do to Melanie last night?"

"What do you mean?" Nick said." I didn't do anything. In fact, when I left her she was very happy. She had a whole new outlook on life. She said that she was going to live for her kids and herself. I stayed late because I was so worried. When we got home the baby-sitter told her that Bruce had called, looking for her. He was asking all kinds of questions. When the sitter told him where she was and who was with her, he sounded angry. She added that before Bruce hung up the phone he said that he would get her."

Nick was very upset and he continued,

"The sitter and I stayed with her until three o'clock. We made a pot of coffee and then she left. I had every intention of leaving at the same time, but we got involved on another topic. We talked for about an hour. She told me that there had always been something missing in her life. There was a void that she needed to fill. It must have been why she always seemed to go for men who mistreated her. She was going to have a new outlook on life and start to be more giving and involved. She said that she thought of the after life a lot. She often prayed, but it seemed to be for the wrong reasons. She would make an effort to change her priorities. She was quite determined to make it work."

"Are you sure that you didn't try anything with her?" I asked him.

"Are you crazy?" He answered angrily.

"I'm telling you that she was fine."

I had a sick feeling that something terrible had happened to my friend. I felt like crying. I told Nick I was terribly worried. I also told him about the call Dave had received from the policeman and I was going to call her.

"Why don't you wait? I told her that I was going to take her and the kids out this afternoon. I suppose I could go over there now on my motorcycle." He said.

"No, I'm calling her up now." I said.

When I called Melanie, a man's voice answered.

I immediately knew the inevitable had happened. I asked to talk to Melanie and he asked me who wanted to talk to her. I told him I was her friend and he said she was unable to come to the phone. I asked him when could I talk to her? He answered grimly,

"She's not about to come to the phone for a long time."

I figured Bruce had beaten her so badly that she was in the hospital. I called Doreen and told her what I suspected. She called some of Melanie's neighbors, but all the lines were busy. Then my phone rang. It was Nick.

"You're right. Something did happen. I just got a call. The cop said he wanted me to go to Melanie's house. He needed to talk to me. When I asked him 'why', he said I would see. I asked him where they had gotten my number. He told me they had found a business card near the phone with my name and phone number.

"That's right. I left it there this morning and told Melanie to call me if she needed me. I'd be right over." He said.

"So what are you going to do now?" I asked.

I'm going up on my motorcycle. I'll check and make sure it's not a trap set up by Bruce. If I don't see a police car, I'm out of there – fast."

A half hour later, my oldest brother pulled up my driveway and told me to hurry. We were wanted at the police station for questioning. He had tried to get me on the phone, but the line was busy. When we got to the police station, the look on Nick's face told me that something terrible had happened. He had tears in his eyes as he said,

"She's dead."

I was devastated. I couldn't breathe. My heart was racing. I asked what had happened. Nick said,

"I drove up to her house and was prepared to make a fast get away if the cruiser had not been there. When I got closer to the house, my heart stopped. Not only was the cruiser there, but there was a hearse. I saw Melanie on a stretcher. They were getting ready to wheel her into the hearse. I was sick and I started trembling. I could just about answer the cops' questions. I was furious and told them that they were wasting their time with all these stupid questions.

"You should be looking for her asshole husband. He's the one who killed her. In the mean time, he's getting away.'

"No, he's not" One of them answered. "My men are out looking for him. You understand that you are a suspect. You were the last one to be with her. We have to take you to the station."

"I didn't care. My heart ached for this poor kid. So I went with them. I asked them where the kids were. They told me that the grandparents had come for them." Nick said.

A policeman wanted to talk to me. He asked me what she had on. I told him that I was positive that she had worn a red dress.

"Are you sure that it wasn't a two piece dress? "

"No, I'm sure. Why do you ask?" I said.

"Well, she's quite a mess. Did she ever confide in you about her sex life? Do you know if her husband was a pervert?'

I almost choked at that question. Finally, I said,

"All I know is that her husband killed her. She told me last night that he would."

I went home and I was afraid of what Bruce might do to me. He knew that I had been with Melanie the night before. I also knew that he hated me. I sent all my children to my mother's house. I went to my room and locked myself up. I cried for the loss of my friend. The phone rang and it was Nick. He told me that they had found Bruce. He had shot himself and he was in his truck on an abandoned road. I breathed a sigh of relief.

Evidently, Bruce had waited outside the house until Melanie was alone. Thank God Nick didn't stay the night. The events would have been much different.

47

Only Melanie knows how Bruce got into the house and what torture he put her through until she took her last breath. He spread her legs and tied them. He raped her, savagely mutilated her, and shot her to death. Bruce made such a mess of her body. That's why the police were inquiring about her attire. No one knows if she died before the dog. He was found shot next to her body. I'm crying as I write this. No one should have to endure that kind of torment. WHY? Was it because she allowed herself to mistake lust for love? for a man related to Satan himself?

The children got up in the morning came down the stairs looking for their mother. As they approached the kitchen, they thought they heard a sound. They tiptoed to the source of the sound. One of the children started to scream, then all of them started yelling and crying as they looked at their mother's savagely disfigured body. Karen ran to the phone and dialed her grandfather. I hope that they hadn't really heard any sound nor witness the murder.

On the night before Melanie was killed Bruce had been in the bar all night. When he left he told one of the guys,

"I'm going home to kill my wife.

The guy laughed. He thought that he was kidding.

After Bruce brutally murdered his wife, he drove himself to the deserted road and committed suicide. He placed the end of the shotgun in his mouth and pulled the trigger. He misfired and blew out the back of his window. The noise didn't make him change his mind. He tried again and this time he succeeded.

WHY ?

...did Melanie stay with Gary?

...did she have so many children?

...did she not insist that Gary see a doctor?

...did she fall into a similar plight with Bruce?

...could she love the men she hated?

The answer to these questions could probably shed some light on the next questions.

...do women stay with drunken husbands who beat them?

...do women forgive their cheating husbands long enough to conceive another child – only to be abandoned again?

If Melanie could have or would have been able to answer these questions she would be alive today.

If women could or would answer the above questions there would be fewer tragic endings in the world.

418217

Made in the USA